Hunter's

Mark

Also by Melissa Snark

Romance

A Cat's Tale

Learning to Fly

The Mating Game

Urban Fantasy

Loki's Wolves Series

Valkyrie's Vengeance (Book #0)

Hunger Moon (Book #1)

Battle Cry (Book #2)

Wolf's Cross (Book #3)

Blood Brothers (To be released)

Star-Crossed

Hunter's Mark

HUNTER'S MARK

Star-Crossed Series
Part of the Loki's Wolves Universe

by

Melissa Snark

Hunter's Mark
Series: Star-Crossed (Loki's Wolves)

ISBN-10: 1-942193-17-3
ISBN-13: 978-1-942193-17-3

COPYRIGHT © 2016 by Melissa Snark
All rights reserved.

Nordic Lights Press
First Edition

Cover Art: *Ravenborn Covers*

Contact Information:
Email: admin@nordiclightspress.com
Nordic Lights Press
P.O. Box 1347
Pleasanton, CA 94566

Published in the United States of America.

The author respects trademarks and copyrighted material mentioned in this book by introducing such registered items in italics or with proper capitalization.

Dedication

To Shael

Acknowledgements

I'd like to express my appreciation to the lovely ladies who provided support and feedback: Sheryl R. Hayes, Rissa Watkins, and Janet Seavey. My profuse thanks to my editor, Marjorie AJ Cooke, and Shay VanZwoll of EV Proofreading.

Book Description

ER Nurse Victoria Storm anticipates a joyous Winter Nights ceremony with her wolf-shifter pack, but a determined hunter upsets all her plans. Daniel Barrett wants her help because he suspects a ghost is behind his friend's disappearance. As a pagan priestess and spirit-speaker, she can discover things he can't. He's as sexy as he is persistent—she finds him impossible to refuse. Throw in a trip to a remote Arizona town, a haunted hotel, and a lost gold mine, and their evening is about to get interesting.

Chapter One

A scream tore across the hall. Before Victoria Storm turned around, the pounding of footsteps and the crash of a medical gurney joined the cacophony behind her.

"Clear the way! Coming through." A male medic, one of her coworkers, shouted the warning.

Victoria turned sideways and pressed her back to the wall to make way for the gurney rushing toward her. A medical team from the ER clutched the railed sides, propelling and directing its motion. It conveyed a middle-aged man in a white t-shirt spattered with red and orange. Blood and pumpkin. Fresh gauze swathed his left hand and one of the nurses mentioned replantation.

She shook her head. A shame—that counted as the fifteenth severe pumpkin-carving accident since her twelve-hour shift had started. In a couple hours, once it started to get dark, trick-or-treaters who'd been mowed down by inattentive motorists would pour in alongside various gravity and costume-related mishaps. Oh, and she must not forget the odd allergic reaction. While she didn't know the statistics right offhand, she would've bet good money that Halloween qualified as America's most dangerous holiday.

Instinct urged her to attach herself to the team but she quelled it. Despite conscious choice, her fingers twitched. Rationality versus reflex. However, her natural inclination as both a registered nurse and a healer ran counter to practical concerns. Technically, her shift was over even though she still needed to punch out. Plus, she had personal obligations that evening.

Ultimately, practicality won out. The gurney team swept past and their voices were lost to the overall din of the busy hospital. Victoria turned and tracked their progress. The scent of fresh blood and fear lingered and her stomach emitted a mild complaint, reminding her that she'd skipped lunch. The scents and sights of the Emergency Room didn't bother her. She couldn't—wouldn't—let it get to her. As a wolf shifter, she'd developed an iron stomach and strict self-control.

Hunger in reaction to a patient's injuries meant she'd made the right call. The second her wolf started regarding people as a potential meal, it was time to log out and head home. Hurrying her steps, she reached the staff room and punched out at 4:06 p.m. She recovered her belongings from her locker, grabbed a quick shower, and changed into a short-sleeve top and low-rise jeans, then slipped her feet into a pair of flip flops. Pulling out a handful of hairpins, she freed the single fat braid that bound her platinum blonde hair. It hung to her waist.

She stuffed her belongings into her bag and ducked out of the staff room just as a couple of her coworkers were entering. They exchanged pleasantries in passing, but Victoria deliberately avoided engaging in a conversation that would further delay her departure. In just a few hours, the whole area would be inundated with restless spirits and things darker still. The sunset heralded the onset of the night of the year when the veil was at its thinnest and the world of the dead intersected with that of the living.

When it happened, sites of frequent violence, injury, and death such as old battle fields, hospitals, and cemeteries were the worst places for a spiritualist to be. Victoria had gotten stuck in the ER once on All Hallow's Eve and she'd sworn—never again.

Tilting back her head, Victoria offered a quick prayer of gratitude. *Thank you, Goddess—I don't have to work tonight...*

Freya's lilting laughter filled her mind. *I can hardly take credit for your work schedule, My Priestess... Heads up— behind you.*

Victoria executed a neat one-eighty, turning on the ball of her foot, and came face-to-face with a blonde woman. She wore a skirt-suit but her body blurred into a ghostly whorl at the knees. Her face bore evidence of severe trauma—massive bruises and broken bones.

"Excuse me." The spirit reached for Victoria with a shaking hand. "Can you help me, please? I can't find my children."

"I'm sorry. Who are your children?" Victoria stepped back, evading the spirit's icy grasp. Her gaze strayed to a glowing white light that followed in the woman's wake. The portal meandered, swaying like a bobbing ship. To Victoria's experienced assessment, the gateway looked frustrated, which definitely matched her current mood. The dead woman couldn't—or wouldn't— cross over until she attended to her unsettled business.

"Their names are Evan and Gail Sanders." Tears flooded the ghost's eyes and her mouth quivered.

"Are they lost?" Victoria asked in a gentle voice, struggling not to worry about the unplanned delay. She'd only had another five hundred feet to go before she made it out the door. Naturally, the distraught dead woman had latched onto the only medium in the entire ER.

"I don't know. Maybe. I don't know where they are

and no one will help me."

"Don't cry. I'll help you." Convenient or not, she would commit to the endeavor even though she had no obligations to do so. Victoria cast a quick glance about to make sure she wasn't being watched. The last thing she needed was a co-worker observing while she interacted with someone who "wasn't there". She already had the unfortunate reputation for being eccentric—she hated adding to it.

Once Victoria determined the coast was clear, she addressed the spirit. "Ms. Sanders—"

"Burke. I'm divorced."

"Burke." Victoria grimaced. "Come with me and I'll check the intake records. Were you with your children when you got—" She hesitated, policing her words.

In all likelihood, Ms. Burke was unaware she'd died. An unexpected revelation could startle the spirit into destabilizing. If that happened, she'd vanish. For a while anyway. But eventually, inevitably, the spirit would reappear, repeating the same behaviors until her presence in the ER became a matter of habit. The last thing Victoria needed at work was yet another recurrent haunting.

"We were in a car crash, I think..." Ms. Burke frowned. Static disrupted her form—a sign of distress.

"I'm so sorry. Can you please tell me more about your children?" Victoria asked in an attempt to distract the spirit. She located an unused computer terminal and logged in using her employee identification and password. "You have a boy and a girl?"

"Yes, Evan is eight. Gail is six. We were on our way over to a friend's house to trick or treat. The children were arguing in the back seat. I only turned my head away from the road for a second..." The woman crackled and turned transparent.

"Stay with me—" Victoria's fingers flew across the keyboard. She entered the boy's name and hit enter, and then waited while the sluggish database processed the request. The maddening blinking cursor... She clenched her hands against the urge to seize the monitor and throw it. If the terminal crapped out and returned a fault code, she swore—

The screen blipped and the computer returned results for the search. Victoria released a held breath in a sigh of relief. "Here it is. Your son has been admitted to the Phoenix Children's Hospital with minor injuries."

"Oh, thank God! And my daughter?" Ms. Burke clasped her hands together in thanks. Her appearance became solid again.

"Gail is at Phoenix Children's with him."

"Thank you, God." Tears streaked the mother's face.

"Was anyone else in the vehicle with you?" Victoria asked, stealing an anxious glance at the clock on the wall. 4:33 p.m. already. The sun would set at 5:37 p.m. and it would take her at least twenty minutes in Phoenix's rush hour traffic to reach her parent's house. Time was running out.

Ms. Burke shook her head. "No, we were alone. My husband, Bill, is still at work. He was going to join us later."

Victoria logged off the computer. "Good. He'll be contacted by the authorities. Now let's get you where you need to go—"

"To my children?"

"Eventually," Victoria fibbed. "Probably, sooner or later. Now turn around. See that white light behind you?"

"Yes, but I don't—"

Clenching her teeth, Victoria reached out and pressed both hands flat against the middle of the ghost's back. Ice shot through her palms and fingers but she ignored the sensation and shoved with all her strength. A dubious bonus of being a spirit seer/speaker included being able to touch them as well, though it was never pleasant.

A startled yelp tore from the ghost. She tumbled, falling straight into the neglected gateway that had been trailing her this whole time. The glowing globe and the ghost collided. Brightness strobed. Both vanished.

"Whew." Victoria huffed.

In her mind, Freya giggled. *That wasn't nice.*

Maybe not, but it got the job done. Victoria resumed her journey toward the entrance. Weariness rode her shoulders so she walked with her head bowed. Although she had preternatural stamina, the sixty-hour week she'd just put in had taken its toll. She couldn't wait to get home. The Winter Nights ceremonies would be exacting, but after they killed the goats there would be feasting—mead and wine, song and dance. Quite probably—once everyone was sufficiently in their cups—a Howl.

Oh, and most importantly, she had the next three days off... She planned to do absolutely nothing but relax.

As she approached the nurse's station adjacent to the ER lobby, the voices of her female coworkers caught Victoria's attention. She looked up. An orderly—Crystal something or other—stood while an RN, Misty Greer, sat.

"...that belt buckle is just too perfect! Oh my god, he looks like a porn star with that thing on!"

"Crystal, shh—" Misty hissed, shooting Victoria a decided *look.*

"How big do you think his package is?" Crystal cracked bubble gum at a frenetic pace with her mouth wide open.

Victoria slowed her steps but didn't stop. Vague disgust circled her... What, was this high school? They were all in their twenties.

"Shh!" Panic on her face, Misty waved a frantic hand to stop.

Undeterred, Crystal continued to gossip and chew.

"Dressed like that, he's either huge or compensating in a big, big way for a teeny-tiny—"

Misty grinned and all but shouted. "Oh, hey, *Victoria*! Are you just getting off?"

Crystal gulped and then choked on her gum.

"Uh, yes." Victoria paused at last. Her gaze shifted between the two women. She didn't know. Didn't want to know. "I have the next three days off."

"Lucky you!"

"Thanks." Victoria smiled. She wasn't lucky. The time off came as the result of careful planning and budgeting her paid vacation days. Her request for these dates had been on her boss's desk—in writing—since last December when the schedule for the coming year opened for requests.

Without turning her head, Misty whacked her friend on the back. The piece of gum popped out of Crystal's mouth and she doubled forward, gasping for air.

"Boy, am I jealous. I'm scheduled to work for the next four days."

"Don't work too hard."

"I won't. You have fun with your boyfriend."

"I don't have a boyfriend." Not at the moment anyway.

"Then you've got the hottest stalker I've ever laid eyes on." Misty grinned and aimed her finger toward the lobby, currently hidden behind the partition. She mouthed, "He's waiting for you."

Brow raised, Victoria turned and moved in the direction indicated. As soon as she passed the partition, she got a clear view of the ER lobby. A dozen or so patients waited to be seen, including a couple superheroes and a man wearing a banana costume. Her gaze flew straight past them.

A dangerous man occupied an entire row of three vinyl seats. He sat in the center chair and manspread—

his arms draped across seatbacks to either side, legs splayed wide. He had dark brown hair cut short and a clean-shaven jaw, and warm eyes the color of fresh-baked brownies. His smile was as inviting as a sandy white beach.

Victoria huffed. She wasn't fooled. Not for one beat of her racing heart. The man was a predator—a hunter from a family with a reputation for short-lived enemies. Wolf shifters and hunters... natural enemies except for an unlikely alliance forged by two exceptional men, one of whom was Victoria's father, Adair Storm. The other—Jake Barrett, the Hunter King. For almost three decades, the Storm Pack had coexisted peacefully with the hunters. They shared the Phoenix Metropolitan Area. They often coordinated their activities and pooled resources for the sake of defending their overlapping territories. The rest of the time, they left each other alone.

Daniel Barrett pushed to his feet, planting his short, black work boots evenly on the chipped white subway tile. He had the tattoo of a black dagger on his upper arm—among the hunters the symbol functioned as a mark of belonging and brotherhood. Aviator sunglasses were hooked on the throat of his shirt. He wore glove-tight Levis that jealously hugged his long legs, and a re-volver strapped to his thigh, right beside the shiny Maricopa County Sheriff shield on his belt which was dwarfed—*Crystal hadn't exaggerated its size*—by a big brass Winchester Repeating Arms belt buckle.

The hunter's intense gaze settled on her and he flashed a bad boy smile that curled her toes. The tem-perature in the lobby spiked at least twenty degrees—a sure sign the A/C had gone out. Oh man, if she could bottle his charm and brew a potion, she'd never have to work again.

Victoria crushed her answering smile, sinking her teeth into her lower lip. She refused to encourage him. Their one and only date had gone well, but it'd been over a week ago. In that time, she hadn't heard from him again. The silence confirmed her misgivings, and she assumed he'd arrived at the same conclusion she had—wolves and hunters didn't mix.

Squaring her shoulders, Victoria marched straight up to him. Trouble was, her diminutive stature undermined the effect; balanced on her tippy-toes, she barely reached five feet. The top of her head only came to the middle of the hunter's torso and he looked down on her, as a matter of course. Throughout her life, she'd endured enough teasing about her height that she'd developed a teensy-tiny attitude problem.

"I need your help," Daniel announced without preamble. He had a deep, resonant baritone, pleasing to the ear. "It's urgent."

"Urgent, how?" She cocked her head and tilted toward him out of sharpened concern. The movement brought her braid over her shoulder. She tensed, mentally preparing to receive a request for off-the-record medical assistance. Monster hunting was a dangerous occupation; unusual injuries a commonplace hazard.

"It's Macan—"

"Macan Guffin? Is that old coot hurt again?" Old Mac Guffin might be a scoundrel, but damn it, she *liked* the cagey Scotsman. The hunter landed in her ER at least once a month, always due to "drinking-related" accidents.

Compelled by concern, she turned away, saying, "Let me grab a first aid kit."

Daniel caught her arm and stopped her. "He's missing."

"Oh?" She faced him again, no less concerned but for different reasons now. The context told her something supernatural must somehow be involved, or he would've just gone through official channels. As a county sheriff, Daniel had statewide law enforcement resources at his disposal. After a moment of consideration, she pulled him into an alcove where they could speak privately.

Intent, Daniel explained in a low voice. "Macan has been over in Granite Creek for a couple days now. The last time I spoke with him was yesterday. He was supposed to check in at noon, but I didn't hear from him."

"Uh..." She cleared her throat. "Not to be rude but have you called the local bars? I mean, four hours isn't *that* long."

Daniel flashed a sheepish smile. "Yeah, I did."

"Didn't find him?" Which didn't mean Macan wasn't there—the man did have one helluva reputation...

"He's not in a bar, Victoria. I'll admit, Macan likes to drink but the man is also a competent hunter. He promised me he'd be in touch no later than two. I tried calling his hotel too. They said he left around ten this morning and never returned. A hunter gone missing in Granite Creek isn't an isolated incident either. I have a bad feeling about this."

"You should trust your instincts." And so should she. The smart choice dictated she put her faith in Daniel's judgement. Although they were only acquaintances—who'd dated once—they'd hunted together on several occasions. She knew enough about his character to elevate a matter of concern to him to her highest priority. His reputation, much like his father's, preceded him.

Daniel stared at her. His face twisted as though he wanted to frown but then he pulled a bashful smile. "Thanks."

Warmth suffused her. "You're welcome. So, do you want to tell me about the other incidents? I presume that means other hunters have gone MIA."

"Macan is the third hunter in the last hundred years to vanish in Granite Creek," Daniel said, deadly serious.

The unexpected information threw her for a loop. Strange. If hunters were going missing anywhere in Arizona, she'd have expected to have heard about it before now. But then, he'd cited a century...

"Three hunters is a lot, but a century is a long time. It's a dangerous profession—"

"They all went missing on Halloween."

Chapter Two

Poise shaken, Victoria parroted what he'd said, "All three? Gone missing on Halloween?"

Daniel dropped a nod. "Yeah."

"Okay, that's got to be more than a coincidence." She didn't mind conceding the point, especially since the matter had just gotten a whole lot more interesting.

"So, will you help me?" He shifted with restless energy. She got the distinct impression that the explanation given thus far had already taxed his patience.

"Uh..." Normally, she'd have agreed immediately. When an ally made a genuine request for assistance, her people had an obligation to honor it. But tonight... Tonight was different. Her face pulled in uncomfortable ways, betraying the stab of discomfort. If she missed Winter Nights, her mother would *kill* her. Victoria wasn't afraid to cross her mother—she did so often enough that it wasn't anything out of the ordinary. However, the prospect of missing the sacrifice filled her with trepidation.

Not if you have my blessing, Freya quipped.

"What's wrong?" Daniel asked, picking up on her

distress.

"It's Winter Nights. I'm supposed to be celebrating tonight with my family," Victoria supplied, although she expected him to have absolutely no understanding what the holiday involved.

"Oh. Right." He rubbed a finger across his upper lip. "That's tonight, huh?"

"Yes, it's tonight. I'm supposed to be slaughtering a goat."

His eyebrows knit but then he grinned. "You've got the strangest sense of humor of any woman I've ever met."

"I'm not kidding. Tonight is important. You need *me*, specifically?" The last thing she wanted to do was dismiss him but realistically, she found it difficult to believe that Daniel required her particular assistance—that no one else would do. Aside from his law enforcement connections, the man must have a hundred hunters at his beck and call at any given moment. If this was just another ploy to get her out on a date, as she suspected, then she preferred to refuse. The gods reacted poorly when not properly honored; she had no desire to incur their wrath.

Pffft... I can hear you. Freya added a rude, quite un-goddess-like sound effect.

Victoria rolled her eyes heavenward. *I'm sorry, My Lady. Of course I didn't mean you. I was thinking of Freyr.*

Don't be such a worrywart. I can handle my brother. Be-sides—the goddess conveyed a thorough up-down of Daniel Barrett that was just loaded with subtext—*it may be you'll find some other perfectly acceptable sacrifice to sub-stitute. Honestly, goats are so boring.*

I'll be sure to mention your opinions to my mother the next time the topic comes up. Victoria pressed her hands to her sides, fighting laughter. She noted Daniel watching her, gauging her reactions. Poor guy probably thought she was mad.

"I suspect the disappearances involve a powerful spirit. I don't have many other options." His handsome face contorted with worry.

"What sort of spirit?" She tipped her face toward him, interest piqued. Ghosts really were her specialty and spiritualists tended to be rare. Maybe his need for her help was genuine.

"Okay, here's the thing... I'm not really sure."

She frowned. "So you think Macan may or may not have been kidnapped by a ghost, but you're uncertain."

"Correct. Look, the whole history is complicated. It'd take too long to explain right now." He grimaced. "And yeah, I know what you're thinking—"

"Which is what, exactly?" Victoria asked archly. She was pretty much right back to assuming he'd contrived a genuine-sounding scenario to lure her someplace romantic. Oh, no doubt some minor but otherwise unremarkable supernatural creature awaited their investigation. After all, Daniel hadn't lied...

And another thought occurred to her—why the hell wasn't Jake Barrett looking into the matter himself? The Hunter King didn't just stand aside doing nothing when his people were in trouble.

"My father's in Mexico," Daniel said in answer to her unspoken question.

"You could've gone to my parents." She sharpened her tone, pressing because this was pretty much the final test. "My mother is a powerful medium also."

"I prefer to work with you." He bared his teeth in an exceedingly wolf-like expression. Direct score: the man had just earned ten thousand bonus points.

"Okay. Let's go, but I will have to call my parents and explain." She had Freya's sanction and the treaty obligating her to his aid. In her head, Victoria tore up her plans for a quiet, boring weekend and tossed the confetti.

Freya snort-giggled. *Please. Who are you kidding?*

Danger girl...

A smile curved her compressed lips. *Who me? Yeah, all right. But that's the polite way of saying it.*

"Just like that?" Surprise parted Daniel's lips.

"You said it's urgent. Your reasons are solid. You're not lying—" Her acute sense of smell would've picked up on alterations to his basal odor if he had. "And we're allies. I assume you wouldn't drop into my work without calling if it wasn't important."

"I called—twice. It went to voice mail."

"I don't carry my cell phone on the floor." She hadn't since the last one had gotten destroyed by an overdosing meth addict who'd bludgeoned her with an oxygen tank. A long story—she really didn't want to repeat it. So she added, "I'm sorry. I usually check it after my shift but I was in a hurry to get out of here."

"I'll explain more in the car," he said.

Together, they exited the ER via the sliding door and headed toward the parking lot. Victoria hesitated. "I assume you want to take one car. I'd rather not leave mine unattended in the employee parking lot."

He nodded. "I'll follow you over to your place. It'll give you a chance to pack an overnight bag."

"Are you sure this isn't just an excuse to get me alone again?" She flashed a grin, willing to joke now that she'd accepted his story.

"No. I wish it were." His gaze ate her up. "And I don't need excuses to do that."

"All right then." She flushed, pure pleasure. "I don't need to pack. I have a go-bag." The rush of anticipation charged her with a natural high. For all Victoria's protestations, her goddess had pretty much pegged it—there was nothing she loved better than adventure.

"You really have a go-bag?" Daniel arched his brow.

"Course I do," she returned smoothly. "Don't you?"

He chuckled. "Your point."

The open road was a pleasure. The muscle car's engine revved as the 1970 Chevelle SS 454 convertible hugged the curve of scenic Highway 89 which connected Phoenix and Granite Creek. The wind noise from having the top down combined with the AC/DC song to create a deafening din.

"For a man who gave me a damn speeding ticket, you drive like a bat out of hell!" Victoria yelled to the man behind the wheel.

"What?" Daniel glanced over at her, confusion on his face.

She sucked a deep breath. "I said—"

"Sorry, I can't hear you!"

When they wanted to talk, they pretty much had to shout. Not that Victoria minded—she hated the strained meaningless chit chat that was the standard fare of first and second dates. *This* was much nicer.

She sank into the plush, white leather bucket seat on the passenger side and dropped her right hand to the underside, seeking the controls. Once her fingers came into contact with the knob, she eased the seat back a few inches so she had an unimpaired view of the sky above. The setting sun cast a reddish blush across the western sky. The stars weren't visible yet, but soon—

When Victoria had called home an hour ago, she'd gotten both her parents on the phone at the same time in a three-way conference call. Unlike Jake Barrett, Adair Storm had no rules about who his people were allowed to date. As a principle, Victoria preferred to be honest. Bluntness defined her personal style so she'd come right out and stated the facts upfront—

"Mom, Dad, I'm going with Daniel Barrett to Granite Creek, so I'm going to miss the Winter Nights ceremony. This is for a case involving a missing hunter and a ghost. He specifically requested my help."

Silence fell, during which Victoria gnawed her lower lip. She suspected an emergency parental powwow was underway, complete with hands over receivers and a heated but whispered exchange. She wound up holding her breath, straining to hear *anything*, while cursing the short-range nature of the bond—an empathetic connection that united all the wolves of the Storm Pack. If she'd been proximate, the union would've allowed her knowledge of their emotions.

"Have fun and be careful," Katherine said with so much enthusiasm that Victoria rocked on her heels and almost toppled.

"Daniel Barrett is a good man," Adair seconded with far more restraint.

"I don't like Jake Barrett much—"

"Now, Kitty. We've had this discussion a million times. He's an honorable ally—"

"I'm not questioning his honor, Dear, only his geniality—"

Victoria winced. Her father was right. She'd heard this same argument more times than she could count. "Guys, please—"

"Beside the point, I agree with your father. Daniel Barrett is a good man. An excellent hunter. He'll make a fine mate and father."

"Mom!" To her acute embarrassment, Victoria squawked and then mentally cursed her lack of control. She should've expected this.

"Don't forget you're twenty-three, Victoria. It's past time you chose a mate and settled down. All of my friends with daughters your age are already grandmothers."

"Mom, this isn't a date! Dad, will you please?"

"Now, Katherine. It's only their second date. Give them a chance to get to know each other before you start planning the handfasting."

Katherine snorted. "At this point, I'm ready to skip the formalities. Sylvie promised to teach me to knit as soon as there's a baby on the way. Victoria's next heat is this January so the timing is perfect..."

The tenor of the engine changed, slowing, and Daniel cranked down the volume of the music. "Why are you growling?"

Startled, Victoria muted her snarl and ducked her head, all too aware her cheeks were hot enough to fry eggs. Thankfully, the fading light provided some camouflage. "Nothing, sorry —"

"I'm stopping for gas," he said and she nodded.

Daniel pulled off onto an unmarked dirt side road that looked like nothing more than an ATV trail. Around them, the landscape remained high desert — brush and thorny bushes. As they continued to ascend in elevation, the rolling hills would give away to more rugged and mountainous terrain.

Proceeding at no more than five miles per hour, he followed it for a quarter mile or so, around a bend. Lo and behold, a small gas station was tucked behind a rocky hill, hidden from view of the main road. He pulled beside a pair of old-fashioned pumps covered in cracked and peeling yellow paint. The place looked like it dated to the same era as the Chevelle.

While they parked, Victoria craned her neck, surveying their surroundings. No one else was around, though she detected movement within the lit interior of the small convenience store. "How on earth did you find this place?"

"Dad owns it. He has a few dozen places like this around the Southwest. You know, so we have guaranteed access to fuel when the world ends." Daniel said it like it was meant to be a joke but the underlying seriousness of his tone gave her pause.

"It'd figure your father would be a doomsayer," Victoria quipped, her tone light and quick. "Why —"

He grimaced. "I need to check in with Jaycee. Give me a sec."

"Sure." She really wanted to ask who Jaycee was but practiced restraint. She didn't need to know all the hunter's secrets. In just a couple short hours, she'd already learned more than she wanted—and that was good enough for her.

While he disappeared inside the small building, Victoria got out and paced around the Chevelle, stretching her legs. Normally, Daniel kept the vehicle's bright red exterior washed and waxed to gleaming. Two black racing stripes ran down the front hood. However, the front grille and windshield already bore a layer of bug splatter—a hazard of desert driving.

After a cursory inspection, Victoria set about cleaning the glass with the Windex and squeegee she found beside the pump. Reaching all the way across required her to lean over the hood, which was still pretty hot.

"Man, the view out here is spectacular!"

Victoria paused in the act of drawing back the squeegee and glanced over her shoulder. Daniel wasn't staring at the landscape. She harrumphed and grinned, but completed her task. She leaned against the driver side fender and watched while he gassed the car.

Daniel set the arm of the pump to autofill and faced her. He propped himself on his arm and tilted so his angle mirrored hers. He stretched his arms overhead, working out kinks in his neck and shoulders. The fabric of his shirt strained over thick, hard muscles.

"So, tell me what we're up against." Victoria forced her attention away from the male eye candy and back onto business. They weren't on a date; the matter of Mac Guffin's disappearance demanded their utmost consideration.

He nodded. "Okay, sure. I'll start with Macan. You know he's interested in his family history, right?"

Victoria scoffed. "Interested is a bit of an understatement."

Whenever she ran into the Scotsman, he talked her ear off. The last time she'd seen Guffin, he'd come into the ER to have his forearm set and regaled her with his notable ancestry. Macan boasted of his genealogy, "I'm the bastard son of a bastard son going all the way back to William Wallace."

"You're a bastard something. That's for sure," Victoria quipped, while wrapping his arm in the cast.

"Oh, you're a mean one, Lassie." He offered her a shameless grin, naming her after a Border Collie without a hint of irony or fear for his life. "Why is it you're not married?"

"Because I've been waiting for you to ask me, you old coot."

"Well, I hate to break your heart, darling, but I'm a lifelong bachelor. Committed to my calling."

"Committed to the bottle is more like." She smacked Mac on the shoulder.

"Oh now, there you go—mean." Together, they shared a good laugh before he took his broken arm and headed home to whatever adventure—or bottle—awaited him next.

Frowning, Victoria forced her attention back to the present. It made her ill to think that the hospital visit might be the last time she'd ever see the hunter. Determination filled her. She swore it wouldn't be so, and added a prayer for good measure. She and Daniel were unified in their purpose.

"Macan's father passed away about six months ago," Daniel said. "He inherited a whole bunch of boxes. I imagine it took him a while to work through the contents but eventually he found his great-grandfather's journals."

"He must've been thrilled."

"Heh. That's one way to describe it." He flashed a ready grin. "The final journal entry supposedly went right up to the day before Patrick Guffin disappeared."

"Patrick was his great-grandfather?"

"Yeah. He went missing when his kids were young. After an exhaustive search, he was presumed killed in action."

"Patrick was a hunter?"

"Yes. Macan's grandfather refused the calling but his father took up hunting in the seventies." He waved his hand. "This was all before my time so my facts may be a bit off, but it's what I recall."

"I understand. What year did Patrick vanish?"

He frowned, thinking. "1945? '46? I'd have to check the logs again."

"And what was he hunting?"

"He wasn't hunting so much as investigating—a haunting." The fuel pump clicked full. Daniel put the arm back into its holster and screwed the cap back on the tank.

Victoria nodded. The haunting accounted for her presence. "And the first hunter? You said three men had disappeared."

"His name was Joseph Briggs. He vanished in 1927."

Daniel advanced toward her. Victoria held her ground until he leaned into the vehicle and popped the hood. Then, she edged out of the way, retreating to the front end. Her experience with older cars was rudimentary but her father had taught her how to check the oil, so she understood what he was doing.

"Do you know the purpose behind Joseph's visit to Granite Creek or...?" She hesitated. Her assumptions were big and blaring. The man may very well have lived in the town for all she knew.

"Officially, he was on his honeymoon." Daniel had strong, steady hands as he went about working on the innards of the Chevelle. For all the classic muscle car's flashiness, it handled like a land boat and guzzled gas like nobody's business. She had to give him credit for his devotion to the clunker, though. She admired loyalty.

"Unofficially?" Daniel tilted his face toward her and winked. "Dad says the guy was an incurable treasure hunter. Any chance he had to combine a hunt for gold with an investigation..."

"Sounds like your father knew him."

"Not personally. Dad is old—" His face pinched and his scent altered in a way that usually indicated deception but could also simply indicate emotional turbulence.

"So, why hasn't your father dealt with this?" She didn't mean the question as an insult. She asked because it was logical to do so. If a long-term threat existed to the hunters, especially in their own backyard, Jake Barrett would respond. Not only investigate, but track down and obliterate anyone who'd dared harm one of his people.

Daniel grunted. "He has—a couple times. He didn't find anything. My theory is that the thing—whatever *it* is—is afraid of him."

"Okay, so it's smart too." She nodded, thinking. Not many spirits possessed the good sense and the agency to be wary of a man like the Hunter King. Few barely had the self-awareness necessary to even understand that they were dead. So this hypothetical ghost—if it existed at all—was uncommon.

"You think my father is scary?"

Victoria focused and found him staring at her with unusual intensity. The lines and planes of his face were rigid as though sculpted from stone.

"Hell yeah! Your father is fucking terrifying." What else did you call a man who couldn't be killed?

"Are you afraid of me?" Daniel's tone was harsh.

"No." Victoria answered fast and without thinking.

"I see." He flushed. Chagrin soured his basal scent.

Oh, oops! Crap! She'd been careless with his delicate male ego. No man wanted to think of himself as thoroughly unintimidating. On the other hand, his ability to deal with teasing would prove a good test of his character.

"Would you like me to tell you how terrifying and manly you are?" Victoria coached her tone, deliberately tongue-in-cheek. She fluttered her eyelashes in an outrageous flirtation and adopted the worst Southern belle accent in the history of the world. "Why, Daniel Barrett—I do swear. You send shivers down my spine and quivers through my thighs."

"Uh." His handsome face skewed like an agitated llama about to spit. He pressed his hands to his sides and shook—struggling against the laughter that got him in the end. Finally, he wiped tears from his eyes. "Okay, I guess I had that coming."

"Yes, you did." She looked him straight in the eyes. "I'm sorry, you just don't scare me."

"It's okay. I think I'll survive." He flashed a big, toothy grin. He caught the back of her head with his hand in a secure grip. Her breath hitched when he leaned in to kiss her. Their mouths touched—his lips were firm and demanding against her own.

Victoria tilted toward him, welcoming his warmth. His amazing vitality. She raised her hands and pressed her fingers to his chest, digging into the firm wall of muscle beneath the soft cotton. He tasted earthy and spicy, like paprika and pepper. And hot like the desert wind on her face. Her insides melted.

He didn't scare her. It was okay—the man still sent shivers down her spine and quivers through her thighs.

Chapter Three

No matter how fast he drove, Daniel Barrett always seemed to have things under control. The contrary part of her wanted to suggest he probably wasn't going fast enough because she longed to see him challenged, but she refrained from telling him. The man didn't need any encouragement.

Just prior to seven in the evening, they rolled into downtown Granite Creek, a small town on the outlying edge of the Prescott Metropolitan Area. The speed limit underwent a precipitous drop and Daniel developed a sudden remarkable respect for the posted limits.

Sitting tall, Victoria peered out at the passing downtown which was mostly composed of red brick buildings with bright green awnings. American flags were proudly displayed every fifty feet. The courthouse square had old shade trees and statuary, and the Longhorn Saloon occupied a center spot in the historic Whiskey Row. Amid the overdone Americana, Halloween decorations added conspicuous splashes of orange and black.

They pulled into a slanted parking space in front of a four-story building built from red brick with white trim. A vertical, neon light mounted to the side declared it to be the Hermosa Inn. At ground level, a row of tall windows ran the length of the hotel. Above it, shorter rectangular windows formed neat columns for at least another couple stories. The most striking feature—a tower sporting a conical roof over the lobby entrance.

"This is short term parking," Victoria said even though it was unlikely that Daniel had missed the sign.

"I'll move the car after we check in." He shot her a significant look—it wasn't hard to suss out his intent. The man *was* a hunter—he must have something conspicuous hidden in the trunk he preferred not to carry through the lobby.

"All right," Victoria released her seat belt and tilted her head back to stare up at the architectural oddity. "That's the bell tower."

"Pretty cool, huh?" Daniel set about putting up the Chevelle's top.

"It's unusual." She didn't actually care for the red brick architectural style that was so common in older Arizona towns. From the outside, the building was blocky. Mundane. However, Victoria supposed she could be charitable. Thanks to the tower, it did possess a certain stately elegance and certainly fit with the surrounding structures in the downtown district.

"Wait until you see the inside. It's cool." He reached into the backseat and snagged his bag—and hers.

Victoria flushed. She strove to smooth her expression even though it was probably too late. Damn, this was embarrassing, but this wasn't how wolves courted. A male werewolf never would've challenged her competence by implying her incapable of lifting a twenty-pound bag. And as a shifter, her strength was superior to any human's, including Daniel's. But, still... She had to be polite.

"Thank you. I've been on my feet all day."

His eyes narrowed. "Am I breaking some seldom-stated werewolf etiquette?"

Damn, he was astute. Her face heated more. "No, of course not. I'm being silly."

"Man, you're a terrible liar." He laughed and she blushed harder.

The entrance had white trim and arched entryway. An engraved metal plaque read: *Hermosa Inn – Designed by El Paso architect Henry Trost – Opened April 1927.* Daniel held the door for her. Together, they entered the lobby. Victoria stepped onto tan subway tiles, traveled about a yard, but then stopped to stare.

"Okay, this is pretty cool," she said.

"Told you." The man wasn't smug at all—oh, no.

The interior had a decidedly Art Deco feel: red oriental rugs, curved archways, and wrought iron chandeliers. Furnishings consisted of patterned wing chairs with ball feet and end tables supporting brass table lamps. A glossy, brown leather couch was situated in front of a massive fireplace that was six grates wide, surrounded by a red tile hearth. An original telephone machine was on display.

They headed toward the front desk. Halfway there, Daniel stopped. He shoved his hand into the front pocket of his jeans, fumbling a bit. "Shoot," he said with a grimace. "I almost forgot."

"Forgot what?" Victoria hesitated, glancing over in question. Well, she'd be damned! Mr. Cool's cheeks had a ruddy hue visible against his tanned complexion. Embarrassment on him smelled like a toasty cinnamon stick.

"When I called, I requested a specific room but it was already booked. So I fabricated a cover story to get the other party moved." He fished a plastic baggie from his front pocket. Drawn in by irresistible curiosity, she bent closer. He shook the contents into his palm—a pair of plain gold rings, a man's and a woman's.

Wedding rings.

"You told them we're married?" Victoria vacillated, torn between amusement and disbelief. On the one hand, she found it oddly flattering the guy was willing to work so hard. On the other, he couldn't possibly think this would help him score points... Could he?

"I wanted the room. It's supposed to be haunted." He shoved the man's band on his left hand. It fit.

"Okay." That made more sense, or so she surmised. "You know most haunted hotels are tourist traps, right?"

"Yeah, well most mediums are charlatans. I'll leave the ghostbusting to you."

"Is this the room Macan was staying in?"

"No, it's a different room." He caught her left wrist and lifted her arm, touching her with the deft attentiveness he showed his car.

Victoria grinned, wondering whether he brought the same concentration to his guns, and pretty much bit the insides of her cheeks to keep from asking.

"Oookay... Where did you get these from? It's more than a little creepy that you've got a matched set of wedding rings, by the way." She didn't want to make a scene, but she couldn't resist giving him a hard time. He wasn't getting off easy.

"I have a stash of props for undercover work." Daniel's face and throat glowed but he persisted, undeterred from his task. He placed the ring onto her finger — and it was about two sizes too big. "Shoot. Your hands are a lot smaller than Cali's."

That name sounded familiar. Victoria pondered, and the vision of a brunette woman in her early thirties sprang to mind.

"Crazy Cali Kinkaid?" The woman had a reputation for being as insane as she was dangerous. Jake Barrett ran an egalitarian organization. Female hunters weren't as common as their male counterparts, but they existed.

"Yeah, we worked a case together last month—" Daniel bit off the explanation. His mouth contorted as though the recollection left a bad taste in his mouth. "Anyway, the hotel has us down as newlyweds. You're just so excited by the possibility of seeing a ghost."

"Oh, boy, talk about irony..." She dragged a hand over her face. If she and everyone else in say, all of Arizona, were lined up in a row in order of eagerness to come face-to-face with a restless spirit, odds were good she'd be *dead* last.

"Thanks for being such a good sport." Daniel smiled, turning on the boyish charm. For love's sake, the blasted man had a dimple on his cheek.

"Yeah, sure." She rolled her eyes and cultivated a sourpuss tone even though she was sure A) her panties had just melted, and B) she was being played.

They approached the front desk where a fresh-faced young man greeted them with a professional-polite smile. His nametag read: Sam Sanders. While he and Daniel exchanged information, Victoria did her level best to pantomime a vacuous bride with an interest in the supernatural. She ended up staring up, out of uncertainty at first, but then admiration. The hotel's ceilings were gorgeous—exposed wooden beams that had been hand-painted in delicate motifs.

Daniel's elbow jostled her. "I said—isn't that right, sweetie?"

Startled, Victoria latched onto his arm with the tenacity of a determined bulldog. She had no idea what she intended to say, but when she opened her mouth, words burst out. "OH. MY. GOD. That's so totally right, my Danny-Man. I'm just like—sooooo excited. Aren't we excited, sugar bum?"

"Oh boy, that's right. So excited." Daniel kept a straight face but his entire body shook with suppressed mirth. Bright yellow exclamation points streaked his aura. He took another dig at her with his elbow but she had a solid hold.

Victoria smiled ear-to-ear like a hungry shark. She

leaned into Daniel, enjoying their camaraderie. Good sense of humor — check. Mentally, she ticked off another box on her list of must-haves in a man. Any guy whose ego couldn't hold up to being ribbed wasn't going to survive Victoria.

The hotel clerk turned away to retrieve their contract from the laser printer behind him. As he picked up the printout, the hotel groaned. The wall behind the front desk billowed outward like a rapidly inflated balloon, and the temperature in the lobby plummeted; a chill draft engulfed them.

Victoria slammed straight from relaxed to readiness. Her wolf surged to the surface. She fought the reflex to shift. She tensed, expecting an attack, while both men remained unaware of the disruption taking place in the Shadowlands.

"What's wrong?" Daniel asked, picking up on her agitation.

"You'll be staying in our Grand Balcony Suite, room 416 on the fourth floor," the clerk was saying, though his voice was far away.

The bulge in the wall assumed the shape of a man cast in plaster, smooth and featureless. His head, shoulders, and extended arms protruded, but the rest of his body disappeared below the waist. His mouth gaped wide as though locked in an eternal scream. With surreal slowness, the apparition reached for Sam Sander's living soul. Those clawed fingers came within inches of the clerk's head —

"Watch out!" Victoria lashed out and grabbed the young man's arm. She yanked him toward her so the ghost's fingers passed through empty air.

Shrieking, the spirit snapped into the wall.

"What —" The desk clerk smacked against the front desk.

"Spider — big, hairy one!" Victoria let go of Sam's arm.

"Wow, you're strong." Sam stared at her and then cast a worried glance about, searching for the fictitious arachnid.

"I work out."

"She does. Victoria is quite the powerlifter." Daniel had to be confused, but he backed her up even though she must've appeared crazy to the poor guy.

"Sorry, I thought it was a brown recluse." Victoria offered a lame smile in apology. "I guess I don't know my own strength."

In a distracted fashion, Sam presented Daniel with the now crumpled room contract. "Brown recluse... aren't those venomous? I'll call the exterminators."

"You should. That was a huge spider." Daniel signed the contract.

"I will. Enjoy your stay with us and have a wonderful honeymoon." Sam fumbled but managed to fork over the keys. "The bellhop will show you the way."

In unison, Victoria and Daniel turned away from the front desk. As soon as they cleared earshot, he leaned toward her and asked in a conspiratorial whisper. "What just happened?"

"Let's just say the hotel haunting is genuine." She directed a pointed stare toward the balding middle-aged man coming toward them.

Daniel followed her gaze. "Gotcha. We'll talk later."

They exchanged greetings with the hotel employee. Daniel passed their duffle bags to the bellhop even though the luggage probably weighed less than thirty pounds in total. She perceived no need for assistance but then, they *were* on their honeymoon.

"I'm going to go repark the car. There are a few things I want to get out of the trunk," Daniel said, touching her elbow.

She nodded to indicate her understanding. With a hunter, *things* inevitably meant weapons. He probably wanted to handle those items personally, unwilling to trust them to a stranger. No doubt, he preferred to bring them in through an alternative entrance—up a back stairwell, away from prying eyes.

In agreement, they parted ways. Daniel headed back out the front, and Victoria followed the bellhop as he led her to the stairwell with a brief explanation, "I'm sorry, but the elevators don't work."

"It's okay." She preferred to take the stairs anyway since she disliked enclosed spaces. Besides, walking gave her more time to make inquiries.

The bellhop took the lead. As they reached the first turn in the staircase, Victoria chose a conversation opener. "This is a beautiful old building."

He clucked his approval. "Thank you. We're quite proud of the stately old gal. She's seen some exciting times."

"I read a bit about the inn's history on the website. Is it true there was a speakeasy in the basement?"

"There sure was! There are hidden rooms and a tunnel that exits through the Longhorn Saloon right across the street. Of course, it's all been barricaded. The hotel only uses the basement for storage nowadays."

The second floor landing marked another turn. "That's a shame," Victoria said, "I'd have loved to see it. Is it true the hotel has a history of fires?"

The bellhop missed a step and tripped. She braced, preparing to catch him, but he made a sluggish recovery. "Most hotels with the Hermosa's history have seen a fire at some point or other," he said, a little too carefully in her opinion. "But you've no need to worry, miss. Our fire suppression system is state of the art. The insurance company requires it."

Victoria considered and then opted to change the topic since the hotel's history of fires was a sensitive topic. She deemed it well worth remembering though. She asked, "Is it true the hotel is haunted?"

The bellhop glanced over his shoulder. "It sure is.

Saw the spirit once myself up on the third floor." He resumed climbing, and his voice floated over his shoulder. "She wanders the halls at night—looking for her lost love. Or so they say..."

"She?"

"Yup. Charity. Poor gal was a guest in the inn the year we opened. Stayed in room 416—same room you're stayin' in." He eyeballed her as they swept through the third floor landing. "But then I guess you know that."

"What happened to her?" Victoria stayed right on his heels.

"Charity and her husband checked in on their honeymoon on Halloween Day in 1927. That evening, he went out for cigarettes. She waited three days for him, but he never come back."

"How'd she die?"

"Of a broken heart..."

"No, seriously."

"Heh." He chuckled. "Charity hung herself out on the balcony."

"How sad. Did her husband ever turn up?"

"No, he never did."

They finally reached the fourth floor. The bellhop led the way into the hall and another fifty feet or so to her room. He used an electronic key to open the door and set her bags just within the entryway. She handed him a tip. "Thank you."

"Enjoy your stay." He smiled in acknowledgement and departed.

She stepped inside and the door shut with a thunk. The Art Deco theme continued through the suite. Victoria snagged the bags off the floor and dropped them onto the king-size bed. She bounced on the mattress, testing the firmness, and then peeked out onto the balcony—two-person patio set, great view, no ghosts.

Within two minutes she'd explored the entire suite, including a cursory inspection of the Gideon Bible stowed in the nightstand. Victoria bypassed patience in favor of restless pacing and even some fuming. She spoke aloud to Freya as she so often did when priestess and goddess were alone. "Daniel should be here by now. What do you think is taking him so long?"

Freya chuckled. *Patience, Victoria. It's a virtue you should practice.*

"Yes, Goddess." She reached the end of the room, pivoted on the ball of her foot, and marched back. "He probably stopped to check the Chevelle's fluid levels again 'cause it's only been an hour since the last time."

Freya's voice sprang into Victoria's mind. *He is attentive. Considerate. Look how well he attends to his lady's needs.*

Victoria snorted. "Lady, my ass. The man is obsessed with that high-maintenance car."

Which means he is qualified to take on a high-maintenance woman... In other words, he's perfect for you!

Oh, burn! Victoria fought laughter. Failed. She dissolved into helpless giggles.

A couple minutes later, Daniel joined her in the suite. He plunked down an enormous duffle bag—the impact produced a clatter, metal against metal. While he got settled, she caught him up on the spirit within the wall she'd seen in the lobby.

"Do you think it's a threat?" Daniel unzipped the duffle, revealing an arsenal of firearms and weapons—mostly knives, but also clubs and a katana. He fished a knife with a staghorn handle from within. The leather scabbard concealed the blade but even sheathed, the weapon emanated a powerful aura of enchantment.

"Probably not. I thought you said we were hunting ghosts?"

"We are, but I like to be prepared. This is able to harm spirits." He gestured to the knife.

"Aintcha gonna show me your knife, big boy?" Victoria employed more than mild sarcasm, but his manner struck her as furtive, as if he hoped she wouldn't ask about it. Which made her all that more curious.

Daniel looked askance at her but gripped the hilt. Metal sounded sweet as it cleared leather and the toxic scent of silver permeated the air. The double-edged blade was long and wide—marked by malevolent magic. Its fearsome aspect warped the fabric of the spiritual plane that surrounded it. The weapon possessed both ravenous hunger as well as its malicious intelligence.

"What the hell is that thing?" Dread coalesced in Victoria's gut. She stared in sick fascination, unable to look away. *Horrifying* acquired a new meaning for her.

"It's an ancient weapon. It's cursed. We don't use it very often." He hefted the knife and returned it to its scabbard.

"Cursed how?" She breathed easier once he sheathed the wicked thing.

"It's complicated." Reluctance hardened his tone. Clearly, he preferred not to discuss it, and she didn't want to know anyway. As noted before—the acquisition of hunter secrets marked forbidden territory she'd rather not venture into.

"You didn't want to have to show it to me, did you?" Victoria's skin crawled. As if the weapon being cursed wasn't offensive enough, silver was toxic to wolf shifters. Pure silver blades were invariably enchanted. Otherwise the metal was too soft to be forged into a viable weapon.

He grimaced. "I'm sorry. I didn't want to offend you."

"Offend, or was it distrust?" Victoria asked in an arched challenge.

"Offend." He fixed a steady stare on her. "I trust you."

Did he really? She harbored doubts but preferred not to express them aloud. Instead, she said, "I'm not offended, but I'm glad you showed me. If you hadn't and drew that thing in the middle of a fight..."

She shuddered to think of what might happen.

He cleared his throat. "Point taken."

"I do prefer you just be up front with me in the future."

"All right, I'll remember that."

When he reached for the front of his pants, unfastening that big brass buckle, Victoria's mouth turned as dry as the desert. *Great goddess of chariot cats...* Was the man taking off his pants? Had all of her prayers just been answered? But alas, he was only attaching the scabbard to his belt.

Victoria sighed in disappointment.

"Have you seen anything interesting up here in the room?" Daniel looked down as he managed his task—the addition of the holstered weapon to his belt. In that moment, the man embodied the essence of oblivious.

Victoria snickered. "Not yet, but the night is still young."

Chapter Four

The old building had a soul all its own, and contained more than one. Victoria sensed them—close but out of sight, lost spirits trapped within the walls. She didn't want to create a disturbance for fear of drawing them all out at once. Of course, ghost hunting was her assigned task on this mission, but doing so while committing a felony struck her as a not-so-good idea.

The third story hallway of the hotel was deserted aside from the two would-be burglars. A "No Service" sign hung from the doorknob of room 302 where Macan Guffin had checked in but hadn't checked out. Victoria fervently hoped they didn't discover the missing hunter within, dead roach-style on his back. For one, it'd be hard to explain how they'd found him.

Daniel crouched in front of the door while she kept watch. Unfortunately, Victoria's gut wouldn't stop rumbling and Daniel's position put his ear level with her abdomen—in the perfect position to hear every gurgle and grumble.

He stopped working the electronic lock long enough to turn his head. "Hungry?"

"A little. It's been hours since I've eaten."

"As soon as we're done here, we can go grab a bite. How does that sound?"

"Good." She needed to eat soon or her wolf would gain ascendance and overtake her psyche. When she started to slip into her animal half—look out. Instinct overtook reason.

"You okay? Your voice is weird."

She hesitated and forced out a quick admission. "I've never broken and entered before. I'm nervous."

"Don't be. I'm doing all the breaking and entering. You're just a lookout."

"Does that mean I wouldn't be charged?"

"No, you're still an accessory." He chuckled when he caught the look on her face. "Stop worrying. We're not committing a real crime. I'm a sheriff investigating a missing person case."

"This is Yavapai County, not Maricopa... And do you have a warrant?"

"Macan isn't going to bring me up on charges. Ah ha—" The light on the electronic lock turned green and it clicked. With a murmured sound of satisfaction, Daniel pushed the door open to reveal a darkened interior.

She and Daniel hustled to clear the hallway. The offensive, combined scents of stale booze, sweaty body odor, and old cigarette smoke slammed her nostrils and she gagged. Her nocturnal vision kicked in, allowing her to survey the interior in the more limited dimensions of grayscale. The room was smaller than theirs and lacked a balcony. Aside from the two of them, it was unoccupied, although the unmade bed and belongings scattered about the room pointed to signs of recent habitation.

Daniel hit the wall switch and the lights came on. An open suitcase sat on top of a luggage stand. The hunter went straight to the bag and rifled through it while Victoria looked on. His inspection turned up a handgun and a bayonet, both of which he took.

"He left his weapons behind. Is that a bad sign?" she asked

"This isn't his primary arsenal. They're just back-ups." Daniel finished with the suitcase and moved on, checking both the closet and beneath the bed. For what, Victoria had no idea, as his inspection turned up nothing of note.

"How many weapons do you have on you?" Victoria posed the question more from morbid curiosity than an actual desire to know. She had exactly one weapon on her person at any given time — a small belt knife.

Daniel stopped and faced her. He considered, perhaps conducting a mental inventory, before answering. "Right now? I've only got two guns — "

"Only two?" She arched a sarcastic brow. He'd taken off the holster he'd been wearing strapped to his hip earlier. She surmised the location of the concealed weapon as being tucked into the back of his faded Levis. His shirt had a tail long enough to conceal the handle.

"One of them isn't mine." He tipped Macan's pistol to make his point.

"Okay, how many knives?"

Daniel flashed that killer — *killer's?* — smile. "Four."

"Four?" Her eyebrows quivered while her skeptical gaze swept his body. Good goddess, *where?* Where could he possibly be keeping that many weapons?

"Four." He smirked and moved closer to the desk. A tall, misshapen stack of paperwork was on the desktop. He hooked the wheeled base of the chair with his foot, pulled it out, and dropped into it.

Victoria stabbed at an empty pizza box on top of the television, but it yielded no secrets aside from the greasy smear. She breathed in through her mouth, drawing air across the sensitive olfactory glands at the back of her palette, and scented the room.

"Do you smell anything?" Daniel rifled through the top layer of papers and picked up a leather-bound journal which he opened.

"Whisky and chewing tobacco." Victoria's nose wrinkled in distaste.

Daniel snorted. "Yeah, that sounds about right."

She followed her nose to where a wet hotel towel was draped across a trash bin. Lips curled over her teeth, she pinched the edge, tossed it aside, and conducted a visual survey of the contents. She refused to come into contact with any of it without sterile gloves. "Do Budweiser and Twinkies sound like Macan?"

"Yeah, that sounds just like him. Anything in the bathroom?"

To oblige him, Victoria leaned into the bathroom and hit the switch which activated a light/fan combination. "No bodies in the tub."

The buzz of the exhaust fan created a moderate din but she still caught his reply. He called out, "Glad to hear it."

She flipped off the light and popped into the main room. "What do you have there?"

"This looks like Macan's research into his genealogy and the history of the area. This is grandfather's journal—" He patted the leather-bound volume and scooted some other papers aside to make room for a crinkled, yellowed map. "And this was on top of everything else, so I'm assuming it's important. I'm no expert, but I recognize a survey map when I see one."

Curious, Victoria moved to stand behind him. Trouble was, the man was still too blasted big so she pretty much wound up pressed against his back to obtain a good view over his shoulder. The position resulted in her resting against him, her breasts smashed against his back. He held up well under tactile examination—soft cotton over firm muscles. *Nice.*

A ripple of reaction traveled the length of his torso. She inhaled, savoring his scent. His basal aroma acquired a pungent punch; the earthy note of arousal. He

turned his face toward her and she viewed him in profile — an expression of wry amusement and awareness.

"Why do I suddenly feel like I'm on the menu?"

"I'm a wolf and I'm hungry. Better feed me soon," she infused her tone with deliberate menace.

He snickered. "I'll consider myself warned. There's a restaurant in the hotel. How does that sound?"

Not quite as appealing as *hunter a-la-mode*, but it'd do. She smiled but regretfully eased off him. Priorities — stomach first, missing hunter second. Okay, so maybe that was a bit screwy, but they had a crap load of stuff to sort through, and she wasn't going to be able to focus until after she ate.

Still, she stared at the map, hoping it'd yield a useful clue. The key bore an illegible scrawl that she assumed was a name and the date — 1865. She tapped the corner. "Granite Creek was a mining town in 1865."

"Yeah, when Prescott was the territory capital."

"You said Joseph Briggs, the first hunter to disappear, was a treasure hunter. Maybe he was looking for a lost gold or silver mine." A reasonable speculation based on the evidence.

"It fits. I want to take all this and study it in more depth." Daniel moved a pile of papers, sorting and organizing, and shifted material to the leather brief case that appeared to have held everything originally.

Victoria got out of his way since it was really a one person job. "What else do you know about Macan's search? Anything specific?"

"No, only what I've told you." His scent remained unchanged along with all the other physical markers she used to judge truthfulness. "The last call I have from him was time stamped this morning just after nine, but it went to voicemail. He sounded excited — said he thought he was onto something. I called him back before ten but he didn't answer." He shrugged. "When he missed his check-in time, I started to worry. I called the front desk and they confirmed he left sometime before ten but didn't check out..."

"And then you decided to fabricate an elaborate charade to check into the honeymoon suite before you'd even confirmed I was willing to come with you?"

A flush crept across his throat. His smile was bashful. "Better than sitting on my hands. If you'd refused to come, Cali would've." When her eyes narrowed with distinct displeasure, he chuckled. "You were my first choice—Cali isn't a seer."

"Huh. Thanks. That's flattering." *Not.*

"Hey, it worked out the way *I* wanted so I'm not apologizing." He finished bundling the papers, maps, and journal into to the case, closed it, and fastened the snaps. "Let's go. Apparently, hungry wolves are grouches."

Victoria blushed so hard the heat overtook her face. *Zing*—he'd nailed it. She'd have to watch her mood until they managed to eat. Grumbling to herself, she followed him from the messy hotel room.

"Do you know his license plate? I saw some traffic cams on the way in."

"Yeah, I do. I was planning on doing that. I'll call my friend, Gus. He works for the Yavapai County Sheriff's Department. He'll have access to those cameras..." Daniel already had his cell phone out before they reached the stairwell.

"Must be nice being connected," Victoria muttered beneath her breath because she didn't actually want him to hear her. She took the descent fast, trusting her natural surefootedness, and reached the bottom well before he did. So she waited by the exit—and listened.

He followed at a more sedate pace, talking with his friend on the phone. His rich baritone carried in the enclosed space so Victoria caught the general gist of the conversation which began with pleasantries, moved on to good-natured ribbing, and tumbled into business—

talk about license plate numbers and BOLOs.

She'd never realized before how hooked into modern technology the Barrett family was, but now she had a clue. They had more than federal funding—like access to law enforcement and, presumably, government databases. The more she thought about it, the scarier the implications. Thank the goddess they were allies and not enemies.

Chapter Five

Daniel concluded his call and they exited to the lobby. A handful of other people were about, including the staff behind the front desk. As they crossed toward the restaurant, their strides matched—short and sedate. By unspoken agreement, they tilted toward one another, sharing an easy intimacy.

Daniel cocked his head and grinned. "So you're saying there's no such thing as a vegetarian werewolf?"

"No such thing," Victoria drawled. "All wolves eat meat. It's instinct, not a choice."

"Huh. I feel so disillusioned..." He pantomimed vast disappointment.

She fought to keep a straight face. "Although, I will concede—organic vegetarians do taste better than those raised on GMOs."

Daniel's foot caught on the tile. He caught himself, did a double take, and then a huge grin split his face. "Oh you're funny."

"Thanks, I try."

When Daniel reached over to wrap his arm about her shoulders, she leaned into him just as she fell into laughter with him. Scary comfortable—the sort of rapport she expected to share with another wolf.

The hotel restaurant was nice, but fortunately not too fancy for their casual attire. They both wore t-shirts and jeans, although Daniel's dress was arguably more formal than hers thanks to his boots. She had on flip flops because shape shifting invariably destroyed shoes and she had no idea what the rest of the evening might hold.

The server who greeted them only spared the firearm holstered on Daniel's belt the barest glance; his dagger didn't rate a second look. Ah, such was life in an Arizona small town. They requested seating on the patio where the black wrought iron furniture and glitzy bronze planters asserted the Art Deco theme. Outside, the temperature had dropped to the mid-forties already. Shifter blood naturally ran hot, so Victoria preferred the cold, but she worried for Daniel. The guy had grown up in Phoenix where it was still in the seventies at night.

"Chilly—we can eat inside if you'd be more comfortable."

"I'm fine." Daniel tucked the leather briefcase beneath the table and took the chair across from her after she was seated.

She dipped her chin and took the man at his word. She counted it as a definite bonus that they were the only customers who'd opted to dine on the patio. They ordered and received their drinks, engaging in small talk while the waiter was within earshot. The quietude persisted for a time after their server's departure, which Victoria found refreshing. Men who talked to fill up silence displeased her on so many levels.

Fortunately, the hotel's kitchen was fast. Their appetizer arrived in record time—bacon-wrapped jalapeno poppers. Five for two people. She always wondered about the idiots who created starter menus with dishes that couldn't be evenly divided as a composite number.

So she tried to eat slowly, but still managed to finish both of hers before Daniel got to his second, which left her hungrily eyeing the last popper.

Wolf etiquette would've made the matter simple to settle, without the need for an embarrassing negotiation. The highest-ranked wolf always ate first. And in the case of a mated pair, the female usually won the prize tidbit because males were conditioned to place their mate's well-being over their own, as well as value sex over food. A horny male wolf with a hungry mate had a far better chance of getting bit than laid, so these matters had a way of sorting themselves out to everyone's satisfaction.

He chuckled. "Go ahead."

"Thank you." Victoria plucked her prize off the platter and downed it before he had a chance to change his mind. She sank her teeth into the middle without regard for the scalding cream cheese that burned the inside of her mouth. The popper hit her stomach in all its rich, calorie-laden glory. Not enough to satisfy her hunger, but it definitely took the edge off.

"Don't they allow you to eat at work?"

"I skipped lunch. Halloween is always a nightmare in the ER. No pun intended." She sipped her soda to cool off her mouth. Her regeneration had already kicked in — in another minute, her burnt skin would be healed.

"We see a crime spike every October 31st." He smiled, but it didn't reach his eyes. Despite that, she still couldn't tell what he was really feeling. It fit with what she'd observed of him on their first date — the man had a hell of a poker face.

"Is your job real or just for show?" Blinking, Victoria shifted her attention to the spiritual plane, opening her second sight. Blues dominated his aura — the shades of balance and confidence, survivorship and leadership. A lot of orange and gold in his chakras. Smoke drifted through his nimbus, marking the dark thoughts he so skillfully kept off his face.

"What do you mean?" His tone remained even. However, his jaw hardened and tightness altered the set of his shoulders. The contraction of his aura interested her more. Her casual question had triggered an unanticipated reaction.

"I mean—your family is well-connected. You have a paramilitary compound out on Red Butte and the National Guard at your father's beck and call."

"And 'beck and call' is a stretch. My father has never voluntarily asked the government for help with anything." Daniel employed humor edged with sarcasm. "He thinks they're a bunch of incompetent idiots."

"So the government doesn't fund you, or supply new recruits or weapons?"

"I didn't say that."

"Yeah, I noticed. You used a lot of words to *not* say it, too." Victoria schooled her tone to teasing but her curiosity had some serious teeth.

He grinned. "Hunters are autonomous."

She tapped her fingernail on the top. "So, let's circle back around to your job as 'sheriff'. Is that just a cover for monster hunting? I know for a fact that you weren't elected into office and your name doesn't appear on any official government org chart."

"You researched me?" He regarded her with open astonishment and grudging admiration.

"You betcha," she said, tongue in cheek. "Right after you asked me on our first date. I wanted to know what I was getting myself into."

He kept quiet, and a grimace working his face. Conflict played out in his aura too, generating spectacular fireworks which ceased when he reached a decision, or so she assumed. Seconds later, Daniel exhaled. "I'm not used to talking about my father or about being a hunter with the women I date. We're not supposed to discuss it with outsiders."

"Right, same here." She bared her teeth and allowed her wolf to bleed into her eyes to reinforce the distinction between her secrets and his. Hunters aside, most of the mortal population remained oblivious to the existence of the supernatural. And shifters, from wolves to coyotes to bears, preferred it that way. Normal humans outnumbered shape changers by the millions, and people tended to kill what they feared or didn't understand.

He nodded and warmed to the topic. "You're right about my job. I don't have the standard duties of a county sheriff. I have my own department and I report directly to the governor."

"And the governor reports to your father?"

He didn't reply — answer enough.

"So, you're really part of the state military?" Victoria pursed the subject with dogged determination. She strove to comprehend it because she needed to understand him.

"I'm a Maricopa County Sheriff. Just not with any law enforcement department civilians are familiar with." Daniel made the assertion with forceful conviction — the title and position must have a history behind it.

"What's it called?"

He grinned. "Officially, it's the Arizona Paranormal Enforcement Squad."

"APES?" Victoria snickered. "Funny, though I can't say I'm crazy about the name. 'Paranormal' is too damn broad for my taste."

"We don't hunt shifters unless there's good cause." He looked her straight in the eyes, forthright in his deportment.

"I believe you. What's it called unofficially?"

"Publicly, we're known as the "All-purpose Enforcement Squad."

"Nice. And ambiguous too. So, do tell — are writing traffic tickets a normal part of your duties as sheriff of the Arizona Paranormal Enforcement Squad?"

Chagrin washed over his face. "Uh."

So, it was as she'd suspected... He'd walked right into her trap and shown his hand. Her smile widened and she closed in for the kill. "So, you don't have a weekly traffic ticket quota to fill, huh? It was quite the coincidence that you pulled me over for speeding."

A bark of laughter escaped him. He grinned, unabashed and shameless. "You're never going to let me off the hook for that, huh?"

"Nope." She snickered again, fought laughter and failed.

"You should. You didn't pay the fine and we're here now." Daniel reached across the table and caught hold of her fingers. When he touched her, her heart jumped like a spring cricket—high and happy. His hands were big and warm, and engulfed hers in a protective shelter.

"Here is nice." And she'd be damned if her voice wasn't positively breathy in a way that reminded her of *Gone with the Wind*, except Victoria lacked even the most basic requirements to be an antebellum heroine. Growing up, she was more tomboy than girly girl despite her mother's preferences to the contrary, which had included years of dance lessons in ballet and gymnastics.

Victoria stared into his warm brown eyes, and lost herself. The outside world ceased to exist. Their auras extended—touched at the edges—blended in an Aurora Borealis of dancing ribbons, blues and greens. His eyes signaled his intent. When he leaned across the table, she closed her eyes and met him halfway.

Their mouths met over joined hands; the barest pressure. Not tentative, but rather savoring. The man kissed with the same assurance he brought to every other endeavor. His lips were firm and warm in contrast to the chilly night air. His breath even hotter, scented with the spicy sting of peppers.

She tightened her grip on his hands, somehow altering it so their fingers interlaced. His hands dwarfed hers so the span stretched her joints to the point they hurt. As a shifter, she'd been born to endure the discomfort of shape changing. Pain always verged on pleasure. A moan built in the back of her throat and she acted as the aggressor. She thrust past his lips, stroking the smooth evenness of his teeth.

He groaned. His tongue met her advance with a caress, still maddeningly restrained. On him, arousal tasted like cardamom soaked in burgundy. He was fast becoming her favorite flavor. She grinned into the kiss, so damn tempted to push his limits and see what it'd take to break that impressive control.

Victoria's sharp ears picked up the approaching footsteps of their server whose stride hitched, probably when he caught sight of them. As hungry as she was, food held its appeal too. She ended the kiss and pulled back. She opened her eyes fast enough to learn Daniel had also closed his. His lashes were ridiculously long and thick, resting upon his smooth tanned cheeks.

After they broke apart, the waiter delivered their food. A companionable silence descended again while they ate. Victoria inhaled her steak—which was rare enough to almost moo on the plate—and chafed at the restraints of fork and knife when fangs would've been the natural way to go. Her baked potato—smothered in sour cream and chives—also hit the spot and even her steamed broccoli was... acceptable.

"Don't like broccoli?" Daniel snickered as she used her fork to poke at a vegetable grown cold because she'd left it for last.

"It's not my favorite." A firm believer in the goose-gander principle, Victoria turned a critical eye to his plate. To her glee, she spotted a small number of cooked carrots shoved aside on his otherwise spotless plate. She schooled her tone to prim and reproving. "You should eat your carrots. They're good for your eyesight."

"So I've heard." He laughed but it broke off. His face

fell into shadow. The corners of his eyes pinched and his lips compressed. Even his scent soured.

"What's wrong?" Victoria asked.

"Nothing—" His head jerked and his hands fisted. With a grimace, he started over. "That's what my mother used to say."

"I'm sorry. I know your mother passed away last April." She tensed because they'd just strayed into what had to be sensitive territory for him. Sarah Barrett had fought a year-long battle with breast cancer. Victoria wanted to kick herself for the unwitting blunder.

"Thanks. It's been six months now. I keep expecting it to get better." His sorrow resonated throughout his aura, a single pure note.

"It will—give it time." The platitude sounded inadequate, but she wasn't sure what else to say. Words—empty without action to support them. Victoria reached across the table and covered Daniel's clenched hands with her own.

Conflict divided her heart. Despite the separation between wolves and hunters, her pack didn't exist in a vacuum. They kept distant but vigilant eyes on their allies. When cancer had sickened Sarah, the pack had engaged in a long, fierce internal debate before they'd sent Katherine, Victoria's mother and their most talented healer, to the Barretts. Their offer had been politely but firmly rebuffed and they hadn't tried again. Victoria's father, Adair, had accepted the rejection with equanimity but Katherine had construed it as an insult and lack of trust. And although Victoria seldom agreed with her mother, this time, she had. The vaunted Hunter King had preferred to allow his wife to die rather than trust his wolf allies of almost thirty years near her.

Distrust and suspicion—that right there quantified all the reasons why her sitting here with Daniel Barrett qualified as a Bad Idea. And she didn't mean in the capacity of an ally helping him locate a missing hunter, but as a romantic interest. Jake Barrett and his eldest son were widely known as being in agreement on most issues. Always, they presented a united front to outsiders. So deep down, she wondered if Daniel shared his father's paranoia toward the Storm Pack and agreed with the decision that had—in part—assured his mother's death. If so, the two of them definitely didn't belong on a date.

She didn't dare mention any of her concerns. In a way, she considered herself selfish for even worrying about such things while he suffered in the grip of grief, thinking only of his mother. Time passed during which neither of them spoke, and the silence grew tense rather than comfortable.

Daniel squeezed her fingers, and then he released one of her hands. He dug a coin out of his pockets, spared it a glance, and offered her a lopsided smile. "Canadian quarter for your thoughts?"

He set it on the table and slid the quarter toward her. Smiling, Victoria picked the coin up and clutched it between her fingers, rubbing her thumb across the rough edge. Briefly, she considered putting all her cards on the table but abandoned the thought. Assumption was plain old bad form, especially since they technically weren't on a date. She opted for redirection.

"I'm worried about how we're supposed to find Macan. Even if we luck out and your friend finds some traffic camera footage, that only tells us what direction he was going when he left town. There are hundreds of square miles of rugged wilderness out there..." Way more than two people could cover alone at night. A thorough search would require manpower and equipment they didn't have. She couldn't help wondering if the smart thing—what they ought to do—would be to call in the official authorities.

"I know," he said in a tight voice. From what he said next, his thoughts paralleled hers. "But I can't call for a search and rescue without some proof that one's necessary. So far, we don't have enough to justify it."

"Are you sure he's still alive?" Victoria hated being the one to make the suggestion but the thought had crossed her mind more than once. They should at least discuss the possibility.

Daniel's jaw hardened and his gaze locked on some far-off point. She got the distinct impression his mind went elsewhere. A hint of magic—tart and orangey—flavored the air. The hunter's mark—the tattoo dagger on his upper arm—emanated a faint glow. Not the brilliant strobe effect from when he faced combat; only a tenth as bright. Following the delay, his handsome features set in a mask of resolve.

"Yeah, I'm sure."

"You know because of that?" Victoria pointed to the tattoo. She wanted to ask why he could use hunter magic to confirm Macan still lived but not ascertain the missing man's location.

"Yeah." He read her mind, because he added, "My father would be able to track Macan with the mark, but remote scrying is beyond my ability. The best I can say is he's still alive—for now." A worried frown pinched his face.

"We're going to find him," Victoria promised with absolute conviction. She strengthened her hold on his hand and entrenched her resolve. Though, for good measure, she added a prayer to Freya and Freyr—and whatever deity happened to be listening—that this evening of Winter Nights would not end in tragedy.

His jaw jutted, fierce determination. "Time out is over. Let's get back in the game."

Chapter Six

The whereabouts of Macan Guffin wasn't so much a riddle wrapped in a mystery inside an enigma. Rather, it bore closer resemblance to a preschool jigsaw puzzle—sticky and smelly pieces, some with their fronts chewed off, others missing... In other words, a real mess.

After dinner, they'd returned to their suite at just past ten p.m. Daniel wanted to comb through all the material they'd taken from Macan's room. He plunked down in the middle of the bed, put his back against the headboard, and spread out dusty maps, yellowed newspaper clippings, journals and notebooks, along with various other miscellanies all over the bedspread.

Victoria watched him, snorted to herself, smiled, and shook her head. It looked like all the thought she'd put into how to handle his anticipated advance was for naught. The man meant what he'd said about getting back to work. A shame—she'd been looking forward to the continuation of that kiss they'd shared before dinner.

Determined to help, she perched on the edge of the mattress at the foot of the bed. At random, Victoria picked up a hardbound book that was grimy with age.

When she opened it, she discovered a black and white photograph of a family tucked between the pages. The man was a silver fox—in his late sixties or early seventies—with a full head of gray hair and a groomed handlebar mustache. He had piercing dark eyes and rigid posture. Although not dressed in traditional Scottish garb, he did wear a distinctive clan crest brooch pinned to the front of his shirt. His hand rested upon the shoulder of a plain-looking woman, presumably his wife, who looked to be about half his age. Twin boys of six or seven years crowded close to her as though fearful of their father. She turned it over but there were no names on the back.

Victoria tucked the picture back into place and turned to the first entry, dated May 1944. The book wound up being the personal journal of Patrick Guffin, Macan's great-grandfather, who had written everything in longhand. Despite being in cursive, she found it easy-reading thanks to his neat penmanship. She needed clues, not the story of the man's life, so she skimmed, sometimes flipping three or four pages. He'd kept elaborate entries rife with details and personal asides. The hunter's cutting wit leapt right off the page and she imagined Patrick speaking the words he'd penned decades before.

Ever impatient, Victoria flipped until she located the last journal entry. She figured the man's final record was the most likely to contain a useful clue as to his eventual fate.

"Listen to this..." She waited until Daniel looked up, and then she cleared her throat and read aloud:

"October 30, 1945. Met an old-timer at the saloon last night who went by DW. A couple whiskeys loosened his lips and he got to talking. With a bit of encouragement, he told me some of the local ghost stories. Of course, the one everyone knows — that widow who hung herself from the fourth story balcony of the Hermosa Inn. He threw in a piece of gossip

about the lady having been murdered by the hotel manager at the time, one Sebastian Greer. Allegedly, Greer staged her suicide, but it was never proven. All rumor and speculation from decades ago. Besides, the manager in question is long since dead, having perished in a fire that consumed the basement and lobby mere months after the hotel opened. The fire was taken as a bad sign by the owners who subsequently sold the business. To this day, many still believe the hotel to be cursed or haunted—possibly both. Whatever the case, there's no denying the Hermosa Inn has been plagued by an unusual number of conflagrations in the decades since.

More interesting: DW told a tale of a lost gold mine, discovered by a miner who, naturally, took its location with him to his grave. Allegedly, and this is where it gets outlandish, the spirit of the miner guards his treasure to this very day. Manifesting as a ten-foot-tall skeleton who has a tarnished brass mining lamp suspended within his ribcage. The locals affectionately call it 'Old Skelly'.

Now, I've seen some strange and scary things in my day, from vampires impervious to sunlight to a werewolf with fleas—"

"That's ridiculous!" Victoria scowled at the journal. She pretty much dismissed the existence of "Old Skelly" out of hand as an obvious fairytale. Werewolves and vampires were one thing—perfectly plausible supernatural creatures. Animated skeletons, however, belonged to the realm of cartoons and goofy Halloween posters.

"Is it?" Daniel burst out laughing.

Victoria looked up, directing her displeasure toward him. "No self-respecting wolf would *ever*—"

"I'm sure he was prone to exaggeration." Chuckling, Daniel waved his hand. "Keep going."

She scanned the rest and shrugged. "There's not much more. It says the skeleton is sighted infrequently, but most often on All Hallow's Eve. North of here, around Slaughterhouse Gulch. Patrick thinks it's 'probably a waste of time but he reckons he'll check it out'."

"Maybe we should too, although, rumors of a lost

gold mine and a giant skeleton aren't much to go on." Daniel glanced over the clock. His charging cell phone also sat on the nightstand. As if on cue, it rang.

He picked it up and glanced at the display. "It's Gus."

"That was fast."

He nodded. "I'm going to take this."

"Sure." Victoria eased off the edge of the mattress and moved a few feet from the bed. She would've preferred to give him more privacy than that, but she had nowhere to go but the bathroom or the balcony. Of course, she could go stand around in the hallway but she didn't want to and wouldn't—unless he asked.

"Hey, man. What's up?" Daniel paused, listening to whatever reply his friend offered, and then said, "Okay, great. Let me grab something to write on—"

Victoria snatched a courtesy notepad and pen, both bearing the Hermosa Inn logo, off the desktop and passed it to him.

"Thanks," Daniel said to her. He held his phone pressed between his face and shoulder and bent, poised to write. "Go ahead."

Succumbing to irresistible curiosity, Victoria edged closer to get a look. He'd written: *North — State Route 89.*

"Yeah, I got that. Thanks. What time?" Daniel added: *11:03 a.m.*

His conversation with his buddy continued, straying into shop talk. Victoria's discomfort over eavesdropping grew in leaps and bounds. The second football came up, she assumed pacing a restless circuit about the room, looking for a diversion when a soft yellow halo caught her attention.

Lo and behold—was that a spiritual glow from the balcony? Victoria squelched an impulsive instinct to rush out to investigate. Instead, she took a deep breath, centered herself, and eased through the door leading out onto the terrace.

This was, Victoria presumed, Charity Briggs—the grief-stricken widow of the missing hunter, Joseph Briggs.

The ghost rested her forearms upon the railing and stood looking out. She was in her early twenties and pretty in profile. She had on a bright red cloche hat with a black feather tucked into the band. Her curly brunette hair was cut short. She wore a sleeveless summer dress: a scoop-neck and drop waist style with a pleated skirt.

To Victoria's surprise, Charity possessed both dimension and color. Often, spirits manifested only their torsos but this young woman had legs and feet, complete with cute, strappy sandals even though elegant, heeled shoes would've been better suited to her attire.

"Isn't it just like a man to bring his lover to a fancy place like this, then just ignore her to talk about sports?" The spirit spoke with a honeyed southern drawl, although Victoria lacked the regional knowledge necessary to assign her accent to a specific state.

Surprised at being addressed first and with such directness, Victoria rocked on her heels. "Ah..." She was caught off-guard and at a momentary loss for words. She recovered enough to ask, "How do you know we're lovers and not married?"

A light but sarcastic laugh came from the ghost. With a flip of her hair, she turned, revealing a face that was lovelier in full than in profile. She had a heart-shaped face and beautiful hazel eyes, bright with intelligence.

"I'm not blind. I've been watching you since you checked in," Charity said. "Any fool could see those handcuffs you're wearing are just for show. Your ring doesn't even fit. No self-respecting woman would let her husband get away with that."

Victoria grinned and twisted the two-sizes-too-big band on her finger. "Maybe we eloped."

"I don't think so." Charity smirked, obviously enjoying their repartee. "Your man is a hunter. He's got the mark." She turned further and pointed, drawing attention to the dagger-shaped tattoo on her upper arm that was an exact match for Daniel's, except a little smaller and hers was silver.

Victoria's mouth opened. Well, she hadn't seen *that* coming. It took her a second to recover. The spirit's lucidity and stability were exceptional, but her awareness of her surroundings? Extraordinary, and unlike anything in her experience as a Valkyrie or a priestess.

"My name is Victoria Storm. My partner in there is Daniel Barrett." She waved over her shoulder, a vague gesture toward Daniel. "You're right—he is a hunter. But I wasn't aware you were one too, Charity."

Charity's slim shoulders swung in a shrug. "In my day, women who hunted were rare."

"They still are. I'm not a hunter."

"I caught that too." She flashed a quick smile. "Oh boy, a werewolf and a hunter shaking up—that's just the bee's knees. No offense intended, but in the 1920s we were as likely to kill each other when our paths crossed."

"None taken. Wolves and hunters—we've been at peace for almost thirty years," Victoria explained automatically. Charity's mix of old and new slang just set her head to spinning. "Uh, my turn. No offense intended—"

"None taken!"

"But how is it you're so damn..."

"Gorgeous?" Charity beamed and struck a pose.

Victoria chuckled. "Coherent?"

"Oh." Charity dropped her arms and frowned. "I wasn't always. For decades, I haunted this hotel. Time was a blur. The outside world changed so fast but I was trapped in my bubble..."

"What happened to change things?"

"A man stayed here—in this room." Charity crossed arms and grasped her own shoulders in subconscious expression of distress. "He talked to me and somehow he made everything better."

"Better?"

"Clearer. I could focus—for the first time since for-ever..." The ghost shook her head. "For the first time since I died, I could think straight."

"How... Do you know what he did?" Victoria count-ed herself as a stronger than average medium and the enchantment Charity had described was well beyond her ability. Her mind baffled, trying to surmise what it might've been, but she came up empty-handed.

"No."

"How long ago was his visit?"

"Um, it's October..." Charity considered, performing the calculation. "It'll be three years come December. I re-call clearly that he visited just prior to Christmas. The hotel puts up decorations and there's always a tree in the lobby."

"Good," Victoria murmured encouragement. "What was his name?"

"He didn't tell me." Charity bit her lower lip and shook her head in a frantic motion. Her obvious distress worried Victoria. The ghost might not destabilize, but if she grew upset enough she could still opt to simply wink out.

"That's okay. Can you tell me what he looked like?"

"No," Charity said, uncompromising in her refusal. "I can't. I won't."

"Why not?"

"He asked me not to tell anyone about him. I prom-ised I wouldn't." Charity looked Victoria straight in the eyes. "I can tell you don't understand, but please try. He helped me, before and after I answered his questions. He wanted to help me move on—"

"So do I."

"Well, I don't want to move on." Charity crossed her arms over her chest. The spirit's aura acquired reddish hues. "I refuse to give up on Joseph."

"Whoa, it's okay." Victoria held up calming hands and chose her words with care. "I respect that. I promise. You shouldn't ever give up on the man you love."

"And I won't. I won't move on. Not until I'm reunited with my husband."

Victoria winced because the odds of Joseph still being alive were just... not good. Daniel had exaggerated the quote-unquote hundred years by quite a bit, but it had still been eighty-two years. The man was gorgeous but maybe not so good at math? So if Charity's husband had been say... Twenty in 1927? She did the calculation. Yeah, the guy must be dead or in a nursing home.

"I know my husband isn't alive," Charity said in a soft voice. "Joseph loved me—he never would've left like that. He was murdered."

"You know that for sure?"

"Yes. He's close. I can *feel* him. He's here—trapped within these walls. I've wandered these halls—searched every room—countless times, but I can't find him. He is here. You have to believe me."

"I believe you."

"You do?" Tears brightened Charity's eyes.

"I do, and I'm going to help you find him. I'll do everything in my power to reunite you with Joseph. I promise."

"You'd do that?" Charity searched Victoria's face and her anguish subsided.

"I would and I will." Victoria held up her hand in a pledge. "Is there anything else you can tell me?"

"Like what?"

"Like... Anything. Start with what you were doing here in Granite Creek."

"We were actually here on our honeymoon. When we checked in, there were dozens of long-stem red roses all over this room... Belgium chocolates on the bed and champagne on ice. Joseph was an incurable romantic." She beamed, love in her smile as she spoke of her husband.

"That sounds wonderful."

"It was. We came here chasing his dream. His fantasy was to recover a lost fortune. I knew him since we were kids, and he never stopped searching. Of course, I didn't actually expect to find anything. I was always the realist. But it made him happy, so we came to Granite Creek to search for the lost gold mine."

"Why this gold mine specifically?" Victoria had no idea exactly how many lost gold mines there must be, but she imagined the count to be higher than one.

Charity chuckled. "Joseph had an old map he found in an antique shop."

"A map could be helpful. What happened to it?"

"When we checked in, he put it in the hotel safe. I never saw it again. A few hours later, Joseph went out for smokes. I waited but he never came back."

"Did you report him missing?"

"Yes, of course, but the coppers weren't interested. They took a report, but I could tell what they were thinking—that he'd left and I was just some stupid woman who was too naive to realize her husband had left her..." Charity gulped air and tears ran down her cheeks. Ruby tones streaked her aura again.

"I'm so sorry." Victoria's heart ached for the poor woman. Compassion welled up within her. She wanted to help Charity, to offer support. It led her to do something she seldom did voluntarily. Victoria braced herself and laid a gentle hand on the other woman's shoulder. Her expectation was that the spirit's flesh would be icy. The dead always conveyed the chill of the grave. But to her shock, Charity's arm was hot.

Charity nodded and swiped at her cheek. "The morning after Joseph went missing, the hotel manager, Sebastian Greer, came by to see how I was doing. At first, I didn't think anything of it. I thought he was simply being kind, but the next morning he asked me to leave. Said he thought it would be for the best. When I refused, he demanded payment upfront. I scraped together what little money I had and it was enough to cover the bill, but Joseph had been carrying most of our funds."

"Did you call anyone?"

"Just my mother, but she was disabled."

"Mr. Greer came back, didn't he?" Victoria had a suspicion—a vision of what had happened next unfolding in her head. But she wanted to hear the story from Charity.

"The next morning," Charity said, nodding. "He demanded payment again but I'd run out of money. He said I to pay up or get out. I refused. He left but—" Her throat worked as she swallowed. "That night he returned. I must have dozed off because I didn't hear him knock—if he did at all. Somehow, he got into the room. He must've let himself in with a master key."

"Are you okay? We can stop if this is too difficult. I can guess what happened next."

"Yes, I'm fine." With a visible effort, Charity gathered herself and then continued. "Greer was mad. In a terrible temper and he stank of booze. He was ranting and raving—calling me terrible names—and saying I had to leave. He grabbed me and dragged me out of bed. I think he only intended to force me out but I fought him. I'd been trained to defend myself. I hurt him but he was so much stronger than me. He wrapped his hands around my throat..."

Sobbing, Charity pulled her hair aside, revealing dark bruises on her throat. Victoria murmured, a soft and nonsensical sound of comfort, and did something she'd never done before in her entire life. She wrapped her arms around the ghost and hugged her. Whatever magic sustained the spirit, giving her substance and solidness, also gave her warmth.

"I'm sorry, Charity."

"I am too. I was only twenty. It wasn't fair." Charity trembled like a leaf caught in a fierce wind. "Afterward, he staged it so it looked like I'd hung myself from this balcony. My mother died thinking I'd killed myself—her only child. It must've broken her heart."

"Let's hope that bastard is rotting in the worst part of hell." Victoria fumed, seething with anger. If she could've wrapped her hands around Sebastian Greer's throat, she would've killed the bastard for what he'd done. She suspected the hotel manager was also behind Joseph's disappearance. Perhaps killed over that stupid treasure map? With so much time passed, it might be impossible to prove. Unless... until... Victoria discovered where Greer had hidden the body. Once he was freed from the walls, maybe Joseph's spirit would confirm what had happened.

"Please be careful. Sebastian Greer is still here." Charity's fingers dug into Victoria's arms; the sudden chill of the grave biting deep to the bone. The spirit's face contorted in anger and anguish.

"What do you mean?" Dread coalesced in her gut. She fought the urge to look behind her—as if the long-dead apparition of the villain lurked right behind her.

"He watches me. He watches everyone who comes into the hotel. He doesn't like intruders." Charity's eyes rolled back in her skull—solid white although the force of her gaze remained a palpable thing.

"Charity—what's wrong?" Chills ran through her body.

"He's here now." The spirit caught fire, burned up, and winked out.

A man's shout emanated from within the room, followed by a whole-body thunk. Victoria whirled toward the sound. Thick black smoke poured through the sliding door. The alarm system split the air with its nerve-shattering shriek. Simultaneously, the ceiling-mounted sprinklers activated, releasing a deluge of water.

Panic jolted her into motion. She gathered herself and charged, shouting his name. "Daniel!"

Chapter Seven

Victoria measured the distance between the balcony and the room in the time she sprinted across the terrace. It took her seconds and centuries to reach the door. The throbbing of her heart. Each labored breath. Endless, awful scenarios in which Daniel died rushed through her mind. Gone before she'd even gotten the chance to know him—and the possibility terrified her.

Her wolf burst upon her with the eruption of snowy white fur upon the backs of her hands and arms. Bones broke, altered, and reformed. Each step she took—an agony. As she passed the threshold, deadly wolf fangs replaced her human teeth. The points of claws burst from the tips of her fingers and toes. Her beast howled for blood. She halted the transformation before it progressed past the midway point, throttling her most basic instincts until she had a chance to assess the situation. Dependent upon the circumstances, becoming a wolf wasn't necessarily the best choice.

For a desperate eternity, she scoured the area, searching for any trace of Daniel. Despite the intense spray from the sprinklers, swirling gray smoke obfuscated everything. It burned her eyes and clogged her airways. Her eyeballs itched and watered like crazy. The inflammation built in her lungs until a wracking cough rattled her chest.

Movement caught her attention. She charged across the room. The bedspread and the research material that'd been stacked on the mattress was scattered across the floor. The smoke got thicker in the center—too dense to see through—so she plunged headlong into the miasma.

Luck was on her side. She came upon Daniel's prone form with such suddenness that she stumbled to avoid trampling him. He twisted and writhed inside the smoldering cocoon that enswathed him—an insubstantial prison. To halt her charge, Victoria pulled up, digging in with the claws on her feet. Her nails pierced the carpeting and cut deep slashes.

A growl built in her chest, overpowering the awful cough that had plagued her since she'd entered the room. Smoke and heat surrounded her, unchecked by the ineffective sprinklers. A swarm of dancing embers filled the air—singeing her face and arms. Her soaked fur provided some protection but the stink of burnt hair was awful.

A pungent odor permeated the area, overpowering the sulfuric fumes. Magic—white-hot and itchy. It set Victoria's skin to crawling in a way wholly different from shifting, stinging and burning like a million ant bites. She snarled at the ambiguous threat, but all her bluster failed to make a difference. The enchantment couldn't be seen or heard—unquantifiable and elusive.

Her frustration built until she threatened to burst. Her primal instincts screamed for her to plunge straight in with bared fangs and brandished claws. She couldn't see or smell well enough to identify a target—and she feared harming Daniel on accident.

Precious seconds ticked past while she assessed the threat. At last, she discerned a shape within the smog — a smoldering spirit. Its hands grasped Daniel's head and covered his face. Fingers made of smoky tendrils pushed into the hunter's nose and mouth as it sought to gain possession of a living host.

Realization burst upon Victoria — it was a wight.

"Get off him!" Victoria plunged straight for the dense mass of the smoke that composed the wight's torso. She swung both arms underhanded, hands angled like five-point baling hooks. Her nails punctured its ribcage and embedded deep into flesh and bone, and corrupted soul.

Wights — rare and powerful. The malignant spirits often appeared upon the demise of a truly wicked person. Their decayed souls continued on in the Shadowlands long after death. But unlike mundane spooks, they possessed the ability to manifest on the physical plane — to touch, and thus to attack, objects and living creatures.

Daniel clawed at the wight, shoving but failing to dislodge it. He thrashed, kicking out, but his attacks lacked direction and force. His short hair slicked against his skull and his clothing was also soaked. Unable to breathe, he weakened more with each passing second. He must be in agony; his distress compelled her to action.

The wight threw back its head and released a piercing shriek. A burst of embers exploded off it — cinders struck her face and arms. Searing pain, more burnt fur. The wight twisted and thrust, flailing within her grip.

Baring her teeth, Victoria snarled and hauled back with all her strength. The spirit fought her but she gained ground — and dragged it off Daniel inch after steady inch. As soon as he got free, the hunter rolled over onto his side, where he remained for only a second while he recovered. Surging upright, he lunged for an object beyond the end of the bed and out of her field of view. She lost track of his location.

"Daniel! Are you gonna give me a hand?"

"Hold on! Don't let go."

"Yeah, easier said than done!" Retaining her grip onto the wight demanded all her concentration. The sprinklers cast a steady rain upon them, but in proximity its hazy aura of soot and heat got worse. The undead thing was strong and slippery—sliding right and left in her arms despite her claw hold. It reeked—rotted meat and maggots. She hung on with grim determination even though the cinders and smoke clogged her throat and lungs.

The wight's head twisted around to face Victoria. Eyes of burning coal stared at her from its ghoulish visage. Screaming, it struck at her face with its gnarled hands. She flinched and avoided having her eyes gouged out. Instead, the spirit racked deep gashes down both her cheeks. She howled in anguish and threw up her arms to defend against another attack, instinctively releasing the wight.

The wight coalesced, a conflagration at its center and billowing smoke about its periphery. It whipped about to face Daniel, spraying sparks which combined with constant water spray to create dirty rain.

The hunter returned like the incarnation of vengeance, the enchanted bone-handled knife brandished in position for an overhand swing. It threw a potent bright green aura that cut through the thick smoke. He thrust it straight at the wight's torso, aiming for whatever heart remained at the spirit's center.

The ghost slipped aside and the blow missed. The deadly silver knife sliced through empty air following an unimpeded arc. It passed within millimeters of Victoria's shoulder—so close the weapon's hunger brushed across her soul like the kiss of death.

"Watch where you aim that thing." She recoiled further, pulling her arms tight against her torso. In her haste to retreat, she stumbled over her own feet.

"Sorry!" He shouted the apology at the same time she spoke. The hunter struggled with a continuous cough that hampered his readiness. Assuming a defensive stance, the hunter performed a tight turn, fighting the smog and shower in search of the wight.

Arms stretched wide, the smoking man stepped out of a billowing column behind Daniel. It reached for his head, no doubt intending to finish what it had started — to suffocate or possess Daniel.

"Look out — behind you!" Victoria took two steps toward him but hesitated. Conflict raged through her. As a protector, her first instinct was to rush to his aid. Self-preservation, however, screamed for caution. She refused to charge straight toward the cursed knife.

The wight leapt and knocked Daniel over. Entwined, man and spirit crashed to the floor. Daniel struggled against an enemy that flowed and fluctuated upon the air. Thick bands of smoke wrapped around the hunter. The tendrils coiled about his limbs and encased his torso. His struggles weakened as the wight deprived him of oxygen.

A continuous growl rumbled her chest. She circled closer, watching for an opening to the wight. It promised to be tricky — she had to evade the enchanted knife. Thanks to his distress, the hunter's movements were erratic — except for his sword arm.

Daniel aimed the wicked blade angled straight up toward the ceiling. He held steady — offering the knife. The exertion of maintaining the posture showed; the joints in his hand were white with strain, and the veins and sinew in his forearm bulged. Rivulets of water streamed along his hand and down his arm.

Profound respect overcame her, not only for the man's astonishing self-control but also for the amazing trust being demonstrated. While the wight sought to strangle him, Daniel chose to place his life in her hands. She must not fail him.

Victoria lunged headlong toward him, her fear forgotten. She seized Daniel's wrist with one hand, stabilizing the position of the knife. With a quick motion, she stroked her fingers across his knuckles, letting him know it was safe to release the weapon into her care. Touch facilitated an emotional connection that astonished her, although it lacked the complexity of the pack bond she shared with her fellow wolves. The empathy flared between them, conveying only the most fundamental emotions—his suffering and stubbornness, her determination and devotion.

Daniel's grip on the hilt slackened. Under different circumstances, she would have assumed he'd let go due to weakness, however, she experienced the exact moment he reached the decision and acted upon it. His fingers opened and the weapon passed into her hand.

The knife's inherent malice pounded on the door to her soul with an angry fist—a lightless void questing to consume her brightness. Victoria gulped and held fast to the bone hilt even while her soul recoiled. She performed a quick assessment, eyeballing the spectral figure of the wight, and took aim. A short, direct thrust drove the blade of the knife straight into the center mass.

The wight shrieked at a pitch that pierced Victoria's sensitive ear drums, adding to the auditory assault of the blaring alarms. Pain lanced through her head and she winced, regretting not having shifted enough to have the high-pointed ears of a wolf that could be flattened. The spirit thrashed in an agony. It cast smoldering pillars off its corpus—thousands of bright embers danced about her. In combination with the dagger's glowing halo, the room lit up like a spooky haunted hall.

An audible crack split the air. The wight imploded, sucked straight into the blade, consumed whole. All its smoke and cinder was also pulled into the cursed knife. A deep pop like a belch followed. Sated, the enchanted dagger lost its green halo and turned silver.

Victoria couldn't let go fast enough. She released it and toppled over. She landed beside Daniel, not too far from the swath of rug she'd rent with her claws. Not that it mattered. Thanks to the incendiary spirit and the zealous fire suppression system, the carpeting would have to be replaced. Never mind the damage to the furniture and walls... A glance around confirmed the fancy suite had been reduced to a disaster area. Oh, and all their papers and maps—soaked. It'd be a miracle if any of it could be salvaged.

She tried to speak, got out, "What a..." before a deep cough wracked her chest. She gave up talking in favor of hacking and wheezing. Beside her, Daniel suffered through a similar fit.

She sagged into her humanity, a sluggish change compared to her breakneck transformation when the fight began. Her claws retracted into her fingers and toes, the wounds healing over after the tips vanished. The plush fur across her body returned to smooth tanned skin. Thank the goddess, she still had her clothing—sopping wet but otherwise intact. She hadn't taken her change fully to the midway point. Her feet, however, were bare.

As soon as her regeneration kicked in enough that she could move, Victoria rolled over and knelt beside the hunter. She went over him with the professional concern of a registered nurse, fearing he'd sustained permanent damage to his lungs.

Panic surged through her. Reacting on impulse, Victoria seized the front of his shirt and ripped through the cotton, revealing his tanned chest which was free of visible burns or bruises. Two words were tattooed over his heart—*Absit omen*. The tattoo burned white hot, still flush with magic. She had no idea what it meant and was too concerned for him to care.

Her examination yielded alarming results. He was unconscious. Soot ringed his nostrils and his complexion had a bluish tinge indicating he wasn't getting enough oxygen. His breathing was alarmingly shallow, his heart rate weak and unsteady. He could still die and without the proper equipment, she couldn't do much for him.

Reluctantly, Victoria turned to magic. She was a competent nurse and she possessed a solid array of knowledge and skill. However, she'd always been a mediocre healer at best. She could heal minor wounds such as scrapes and bruises, and broken bones so long as the fracture was clean. Internal injuries defied her ability beyond the most rudimentary assessment.

"Freya, please, help me—help him." Offering up a heartfelt prayer, Victoria turned to her goddess. She pressed her hands flat against his sides, beneath his diaphragm, and gathered the energy necessary to weave a restoration spell. A soft glow emanated from her palms and—she knew from experience—her eyes and mouth also emitted the same light. The magic connected her life pattern to Daniel's, allowing her to extend her awareness so she perceived the damage to the lining of his respiratory tract—swelling and airway collapse.

Freya's answer came as a deluge of divinity that surged into Victoria. No words—only pure power. The mystical halo she mustered on her own increased a hundredfold and strobed with the brilliance of a nova. The goddess lifted her priestess on an exhilarating high, granting a tantalizing glimpse of wondrous things beyond mortal comprehension.

Thank you. Thank you. With profuse gratitude, Victoria grabbed hold of the primal essence as best she was able and channeled it into Daniel, infusing the hunter with the curative magic. Her effort bathed him in radiant light.

You are most welcome, My Priestess.

Uttering a soft cry, Victoria bent and covered Daniel's mouth with her own in a life-giving kiss. The firm press of their lips allowed her to better direct the healing spell to where it was most needed. With Freya's assistance, it required less than a minute to accomplish what would've taken her hours alone.

The kiss turned sensual, a caress rather than a curative. Abruptly, Victoria became aware of the press of Daniel's hands against the back of her head. She rested atop him with her breasts flattened against the hard wall of his chest. Her hands still gripped his sides but the magic had ceased.

Stunned, she lifted her face to stare into his sleepy gaze. Bedroom eyes. Daniel was aware and alert—and he would be okay. Thrilled and relieved all at once, she offered him a stupid smile.

Unfortunately, the fire alarm and the sprinkler spray continued unabated. She yelled to be heard over the din. "Are you okay?"

"Yeah, I'm okay," Daniel shouted in return. "Thanks to you."

Heat suffused her face. Overcome with inexplicable shyness, Victoria slithered off his chest and plunked down cross-legged on the sodden carpet beside him. He also sat up, glanced around, and scooted over to grab his scary-ass knife. As soon as he returned the dagger to its scabbard, the thing's terrifying presence was muted.

Victoria breathed a sigh. "It's really Freya you should thank."

Daniel hesitated and a quicksilver reaction swept over him, rendering his expression unreadable. She halfway expected him to refute Freya's involvement or existence. Few people believed in the old gods or even demonstrated the courtesy of polite tolerance. Of course, Daniel wasn't an ordinary man. For one, he fought monsters for a living.

"Thank you, Freya." He dipped his head in a show

of respect.

Tell him he is welcome, Freya said. His appreciation pleased the goddess. More than that, she approved of his ready acknowledgement of her existence. So intimate was the bond between priestess and goddess that Victoria experienced Freya's pleasure as though the emotion was her own.

"She says you're welcome." Belatedly, it occurred to Victoria that she'd just broken one of her people's strictest rules against using their magic to help outsiders. Her healing was only meant for other wolf shifters and their human and wolf kinfolk. The realization rendered her stunned—she'd never before made a mistake this huge.

Before Victoria managed to compose an apology, Freya spoke again, *I do not object to having helped him. He is your ally and he fought well even though he was overcome by the wight. Healing him was appropriate and honorable.*

"Thank you, Goddess," Victoria said, speaking quietly enough that she wouldn't be overheard over the constant, and now annoying, blare of the alarm. And hell—wasn't someone going to do something about the blasted sprinklers? She was sick to death of getting drenched.

Freya snorted quite indelicately. *That won't be a problem much longer.*

A great boom detonated cracked wood and the door to the room exploded inward. Firemen clad in full emergency gear burst into the honeymoon suite.

"Oh yeah," Victoria muttered. "We're being rescued."

Chapter Eight

A dozen different emergency vehicles ranging from police cruisers to fire engines occupied the street in front of the hotel. Traffic cones and cops redirected the few passing vehicles. All the hotel occupants congregated in clusters while a mix of uniformed officers and hotel security stood watch over the unhappy crowd. Most of the guests were disheveled as a consequence of having been dragged out of bed. Following the fire alarm, the entire hotel had been evacuated while safety crews performed a thorough inspection of the property.

"Okay, Victoria. That's everything I needed to know." Officer Sims flipped his report pad closed.

"Are we done then?" A wave of heartfelt relief swept her to have the uncomfortable interview finally over. Throughout, she'd stuck to the cover story she and Daniel had hastily constructed—a fire had started in their room, setting off the alarm and sprinkler system. She didn't know the cause of the fire but if pressed to speculate, maybe bad wiring had been at fault?

"We're done. If there's anything else I can do for you..." His gaze lingered on her—an interest that had nothing to do with his job and everything to do with the way her wet t-shirt clung to her breasts.

"Thank you, but no." She offered a polite smile in rebuff. Although there were things the police officer could've obtained that she needed, such as a dry set of clothes. After an hour in the back of the ambulance beneath a thermal blanket, her shirt and jeans were still soggy.

On cue, an EMT with the ambulance crew appeared from around the side of the vehicle. Jerome—early-thirties, handsome, dark hair, and brown skin. He halted. His hostile regard flickered to Officer Sims. He raised his arm; a pair of plastic flip-flops dangled from his fingers. "I found a pair of sandals for you. They may be a bit big."

"I'm sure they'll be fine. Thank you." Standing between the two men, she set the shoes on the ground and slipped her feet into them. As predicted, they were a couple sizes too large but she didn't care—better than going barefoot. Now she just needed to find her missing companion and—

Through convenient coincidence, Daniel approached from the direction of the hotel. He wore his sheriff's badge in plain sight on his belt—the credential that allowed him to move among the other officials but then hesitated, frowning at the two men who'd been hovering over her for the last half hour. She suppressed a snort—served him right for disappearing on her.

"Oh, I see my husband. Thanks guys! You've been terrific." Victoria slipped between them and made a bee-line for Daniel.

"Sorry for leaving you alone for so long. I had to run interference with the local police." Daniel settled his hand against the small of her back. The hunter had acquired a clean shirt, but she caught the distinct odor of wet denim. He must be at least as uncomfortable as she was.

"No problem. I understand." She hesitated, pondering. "I think I have a lead on locating Mac."

"Yeah?" He lit with feline intensity. A question trembled on his lips, but he held it and followed her, demonstrating an impressive combination of self-discipline and trust. "That's great. All those old papers are probably ruined. Even if something survived, I doubt we'll be able to get back into the suite anytime soon. There's an arson investigator on the scene."

Victoria winced. "Do they think we...?"

"Maybe... But even if they do, don't worry about it." He shrugged. "My family has enough influence it won't stick."

She pressed her lips together in a grim line and bit her tongue. His family might have sway, but hers didn't. Arson charges could ruin her career. But no, he'd trusted her with his life during the fight with the wight. She owed it to him to believe he would put the same effort into defending her as he would himself.

"Hey." Daniel brushed his fingers across the inside of her elbow. His touch elicited a visceral reaction—electrified her skin—so every hair stood on end. His voice was a caress. "You know I've got your back?"

"Yeah, I know." A smile split her mouth. Joy suffused her heart. Of its own volition, her hand snagged his in a tight grip. She swung their linked arms in a gesture of unity.

Her smile faded, and she hesitated for a moment, considering. Everything she owned except the clothing she wore was currently inaccessible—at home in Phoenix or up in the hotel room. Daniel only had the weapons he carried on his person, which happened to include the wicked knife—a questionable blessing or curse.

"Where are we going?" Daniel shortened his long stride to match hers.

"Over to the Longhorn Saloon." From the look of it,

the bar was still open. No matter, she hurried her steps, concerned it would close its doors at midnight since it was a weeknight. Outside of the college towns, small Arizona cities seldom had much nightlife.

"All right."

She let go of his hand and headed toward the corner at the closest stoplight. He turned, observing her progress. Maybe he expected her to wait or look back. She kept going and had the gratification of his rushed steps as he kicked it into high gear. Daniel caught up with her on the corner. When the walk sign lit, they crossed together.

"Do you have your lock picks on you?"

"Right here." He patted his pocket.

"Good. We're going to need them."

"Man, you just love the mysterious lead-in, don't you?"

Victoria only smiled.

They entered the Longhorn Saloon and paused within the entryway to survey the area. The bar was crowded with unkempt refugees from the Hermosa Inn. Apparently, others had shared their idea to refuge there. It made blending in far easier. They worked their way to the rear of the establishment where the restrooms were located in a short, dingy hallway. Just past it, a third door bore an "Employees Only" sign.

She traded a look with Daniel—understanding without words. He turned to stand watch. Victoria grabbed the handle, gave it a quick twist, and found it unlocked.

"Come on, let's go." She shoved it open, ducked inside, and Daniel followed her. She shut the door again, plunging them into darkness. Of course, her nocturnal vision compensated, so she could see just fine. The area wasn't totally dark—some light seeped in through high, narrow windows.

"Ah, I think I have a penlight somewhere." Daniel

fumbled with his pockets. He bumped his elbow into her shoulder, muttered an apology, and kept searching.

Temptation pushed her tongue into her cheek. She came *this close* to lending him a hand with the pat down of his jeans. Propriety, however, got the better of her. They had higher priorities than a game of slap and tickle.

"Does this help?" Victoria allowed her eyes to shift fully to wolf so they cast a warm golden glow sufficient to illuminate the area.

"Yeah, thanks." He flashed a ready grin. "You're handier than a flashlight."

She snorted. "Gee, thanks. You know just what to say to flatter a girl."

"You're brilliant."

"Oh, a witty pundit..." She groaned and took the lead along the hallway. Her altered vision lit the way. She passed a light switch without flipping it because she preferred not to risk attracting any attention to their trespass.

"So are you gonna tell me where we're going?"

"Yes. In the 1920s, the Hermosa Inn had a speakeasy located in the basement. The bellhop told me there's a secret tunnel in the basement that leads to the—"

He snapped his fingers. "The Longhorn Saloon."

"Correct." She grinned, glancing over her shoulder.

Within a minute, they located the door leading to the basement—it was locked. Without being asked, Daniel extracted his lock picks and set to work. To Victoria's amusement, he got it open a lot faster than the electronic lock from earlier—a good thing because the prospect of getting caught caused her nothing but anxiety. She just wasn't cut out for life as a criminal.

"Second time's the charm?" Victoria quipped when the tumblers rolled.

He grunted, less than amused. "I don't have as much experience with electronic locks."

"Because that's not covered in cop school?" She poked him in the side and followed right on his heels.

"Not so much." Daniel chuckled and pushed the reinforced steel fire door open. Victoria slipped past him and headed down. Her glowing eyes once again lit the way.

"So spill... what's up?" Daniel's voice echoed as did their footsteps. "Why are we heading to the Inn's basement? I expect you weren't overcome by a burning desire to check out the old speakeasy."

"Not quite." Chuckling, she launched into a quick explanation. "Before you were attacked, I spoke with Charity Briggs out on the balcony."

"Yeah? That's great. What'd she say?"

She paused on the turn, midway down. The explanation would take a minute. She preferred to provide it all upfront even if it meant stopping for a second. "Charity believes her husband's soul is trapped somewhere inside the hotel. She says she can feel Joseph. She's searched but hasn't been able to find him. She also identified the murderer of both herself and her husband as Sebastian Greer, the original hotel manager."

"Sebastian Greer died in a hotel fire," Daniel mused. "He was the thing that attacked us?"

"His soul became a wight—the smoldering spirit." Victoria summarized her conversation with Charity, electing to leave a great deal out because they were pressed for time. Later, after this was all over, she would provide him with an exact accounting of the details.

Daniel construed his own conclusion. "So you think Greer killed Joseph and hid his body somewhere in the basement?"

"Yeah, I do—probably sealed up inside the walls or the foundation since it was never found. Remember that spirit I observed trapped within the lobby wall?"

"That was Joseph?"

Victoria bobbed her head. "I believe he needs our

help—that he's reaching out for it but he's unable to manifest entirely on the ground level. Meanwhile, Charity's been searching for her husband's soul for decades but she can't find him because she can't descend past the lobby."

"Their souls have been separated by a single story for almost a century?"

"And by Greer's wight," Victoria added, determined to assign blame where it was due. She derived vicious satisfaction from the knowledge that the bastard's soul had been destroyed. He'd never hurt anyone ever again.

"Man, that's fucked up." Daniel looked as though he'd been floored by the revelation.

"Did you know Charity was a hunter too?"

His brow knit and he hesitated. "No, no idea. I'll ask my father about it when I get a chance."

She nodded, satisfied with his answer. "I'm hoping when we free Joseph's spirit, he can tell us the location of the lost gold mine. C'mon, let's get moving. Mac Guffin isn't going to save himself."

Victoria took the last steps with the hunter hot on her heels. It took some searching but eventually they located the entryway to the old tunnel along the foundation wall facing the Hermosa Inn. Daniel scrounged a crowbar which he used to pry off the boards. The rusted hinges stuck. He put his shoulder against it and forced it open wide enough to allow them to pass. She slipped through the narrow opening easily but he had to turn sideways to squeeze his broad shoulders through. He brought the crowbar along—no doubt a smart precaution.

The tunnel on the other side was cool and pitch black—a narrow concrete corridor with a low ceiling that forced Daniel to stoop. Once again, her eyes cast the glow that served as their only illumination, but even with that they could only see a few feet ahead. Victoria hovered close to Daniel's side while they advanced. The attack in the hotel room had left her on edge and feeling protective—maybe even overprotective—of the man she'd come to regard as her hunting partner. The attitude was dangerously close to pack mentality—she'd have to watch that.

"I expected it to smell worse," Daniel said.

"So did I." She sniffed and inhaled dust. A sharp sneeze tore from her. At least she didn't detect any vermin or mold.

"It's been sealed up on both sides for a long time."

It took less than a minute to reach the other side of the tunnel. They encountered another entrance, presumably leading to the basement of the Hermosa Inn. She stood guard while Daniel pried the door open. This time, at least, it wasn't boarded shut on the inside. Here, the hallway widened and the ceiling height rose—the dustiness decreased too. The janitorial staff maintained a commendable level of cleanliness. Oh, and it kept getting better—they came across a light switch on the wall. Victoria swatted it—ceiling mounted lights came on.

"Sweet. How do you intend to figure out where the body is hidden?" Daniel asked. "I've worked with cadaver dogs, but Joseph has been dead for decades..."

"Are you calling me a dog?" Victoria endeavored to sound deliberately snappy.

"Uh." He gave a guilty start and glanced at her face. As soon as he took in her wicked smile, he lapsed into a double take. Snickering, he said, "Very funny."

She grinned. "My nose is good but nowhere close to a cadaver dog's."

"No?" He looked askance at her, clearly doubtful.

"No." She offered the affirmation, one hundred percent serious. Domesticated dogs actually possessed superior olfactory abilities to wolves—canines having been bred for it. Oh, her sense of smell far surpassed that of any human, but she couldn't have given the average bloodhound a run for the money. It didn't matter—her plan for locating the site of Joseph's grave had nothing to do with any of the *five* mundane senses.

"Huh." He gave the distinct impression of filing away the information for future use. After a delay, he asked, "What's the plan?"

"Joseph's been trying to reach out to me since we arrived. Hopefully, now that Greer's out of the picture, he'll be able to break through." Victoria closed her eyes and focused on opening her inner eye so she could peer into the Shadowlands. While she always had some awareness of the spiritual plane—particularly auras—it operated in degrees.

"So we're gonna let him find us? I hope he's in a congenial mood." Daniel grumbled, and his underlying scent remained tart with uneasiness.

"Me too." Worry ate at her also to a lesser extent, but she hadn't forgotten Macan. When she opened her eyes, she perceived more of the otherworld than the physical. Cupping her hands to her mouth, she called, "Joseph! It's all right to come out now. Sebastian Greer is gone..."

She advanced along the hall, watching for any spiritual activity along the walls, and Daniel came with her. They progressed as a team—side by side. Her position allowed her to guard against any incoming threats from the left while he parried to the right. If attacked from two sides, they could shift stances so they were back to back. Every thirty feet, Victoria repeated her summons. Still, long minutes dragged past without anything to show for their efforts. Patience wasn't her strong suit—never had been. Frustration rumbled in her throat.

"Easy." Daniel's deep blue nimbus washed over her—cool and comforting as the ocean. He centered her.

She glanced over, opening her mouth to speak when the wall beside her rippled and bubbled. A hand sprouted toward her, supported on a thin arm stalk. With an exclamation, Victoria jerked toward it.

Daniel mirrored her motion. "What is it?"

"I think we've found Joseph." Or, more accurately, Joseph had found them. She refrained from grabbing the ghost's arm. Spirits were notoriously skittish—sudden movement might startle him into vanishing.

Where the arm joined the wall, the smooth gray surface ballooned outward, and became two distinct lumps—his head and other hand. His face resembled that of a mannequin, mouth open wide in a perpetual silent scream. A man trapped beneath a sheet except his prison was constructed of concrete.

"That's it. Let me help you." Cautiously, Victoria reached for his hand. Just before their fingertips touched, the spirit's entire body thinned and quivered like a rubber band strained to its breaking point. Quicksilver swift, he snapped back into the wall and vanished.

"No!" Victoria lunged, but her palms smacked against the solid surface. She pounded it with her fists. "Damn it! Come back."

"Victoria?" Daniel touched her shoulder.

"What?" The inquiry burst from her, rude and abrupt, a measure of her immense frustration. She remained faced away from him.

"Look."

She turned—stopped. Her lips parted in sheer surprise. Charity Briggs stood at the end of the hallway, as solid as could be. She wore her bright red cloche hat and summer dress, looking as though she'd stepped straight out of a 1920s' fashion magazine.

"Now that Greer is gone, I'm finally able to enter the basement," Charity explained in answer to Victoria's unvoiced question.

"How is it I can see her?" Daniel asked from the side of his mouth.

"I don't know." Victoria shook her head—it didn't matter. The fact that he could was remarkable enough. "Maybe because it's Winter Nights—All Hallow's Eve? The veil is at its thinnest. Spirits are often able to cross over."

He grunted, signaling acceptance.

Charity turned away and addressed them over her shoulder. "I know where Joseph is trapped. Follow me."

Daniel and Victoria traded a quick glance—agreement resonated between them. They chased after Charity, fast at first, but then slowing once they'd caught up. The spirit led them down the hallway, around a corner, and then walked straight through a closed door.

Victoria grabbed the knob and said a silent prayer of thanks to find it unlocked. They entered an immense room that housed the hotel's central heating and air conditioning. Just past the entryway, they paused to get oriented.

"Over here." Charity's voice carried from somewhere beyond the furnace. They circled and found the ghost standing along the far wall before a charred section of concrete three feet in diameter. The blackened swath pulsated and festered, oozing discolored pus.

"Do you see that?" Victoria pointed.

"See what?" Daniel asked in a pinched-brow voice.

Victoria forced her vision back to the material plane. As she suspected, the wall was smooth and unblemished. Daniel couldn't perceive the phenomenon because it existed only in the Shadowlands. Blinking restored her second sight. She stepped up to the wall and placed her hand over the discoloration.

"We want to dig here."

"Give me some space." Daniel stepped up, hefting the crowbar into position. His biceps bulged, forearms rippled, the clean play of sinew beneath his tanned skin.

"Okay." Nodding, Victoria stepped aside. Of course, she could have utilized her claws to rip into the concrete, but the area was too small for both of them to work safely. Ultimately, the metal bar was the superior tool for the job. Besides, laziness suited her mood. The fight against the wight had worn her out. Let Daniel do some of the heavy lifting this time.

With a grunt of exertion, Daniel swung the crowbar, a stroke that embedded the pronged end deep in the concrete. The blow sent up a fine dust and a spray of pebbles. When he yanked the bar free, larger chunks of rubble tumbled to the floor. He set a hard, steady rhythm, toiling at the task.

Charity pressed a clenched fist to her mouth and sank her teeth into her finger. She trembled, and anxiety rolled off her in waves.

"It's going to be okay. Just a few more minutes and you'll be reunited with your husband." Seeking to comfort the other woman, Victoria reached over and took Charity's hand. The spirit glanced at her in clear surprise but didn't withdraw.

"It's just been so long... I can't believe it's finally over. We're going to be together again at last." Teary-eyed, Charity sniffled and tightened her grip on Victoria's hand.

The two women stood together while Daniel worked. A slick sheen of sweat shone on his skin. He widened the hole to about two feet across, and then he focused on deepening it. Debris formed a pile on the floor. On a final swing, the sound of the strike changed—a dull, hollow impact—and over half the crowbar sank into the opening.

Changing his grip on the handle, Daniel hauled back on the crowbar and extracted it amid a shower of rubble. He dropped the tool to the floor where it landed with a clatter. Still breathing hard, he rested his hand alongside the hole and stared inside.

"What do you see?" An excited quiver shot through Victoria and she released Charity's hand. It required all her self-control not to rush closer for a better look.

"It's dark—I can't see anything." He squinted and cocked his head while he performed a pat down of his pants.

"Let me." Unable to stand it any longer, Victoria pressed closer. Daniel yielded, stepping aside so she had a clear view. As he'd said, it was dark. She caught a charcoal scent that reminded her of an old fire pit.

"Here." Daniel produced the elusive pen light he'd been unable to locate earlier. He passed it to Victoria over her shoulder.

"Thanks. I think I see something." She aimed the beam of light into the interior, illuminating what she thought was a burnt board. She reached in to remove it, but then her mind connected the dots. That wasn't a piece of wood, but rather a charred bone. Hastily, she jerked her arm back.

Something moved inside the wall.

"Charity." Victoria beckoned for the spirit.

"What can I do?" Charity hurried closer and gazed through the pit. A cry fell from her lips. Without waiting for instructions, she walked into the wall—the front half of her body vanished into the concrete. When she stepped back, Charity drew a man—presumably Joseph—along with her. The couple was locked in a lover's embrace, a passionate kiss that went on and on.

At first, a stupid smile overtook Victoria. She indulged the exhilaration—stealing a glance at Daniel, she found the hunter grinning like mad. He caught her looking at him. Their gazes locked and the triumph became theirs. Together, they'd accomplished this amazing thing—tormented lovers separated by centuries, reunited at last. When he raised his arm in an unspoken invitation, she pressed close to his side, and he wrapped his hand around her waist. They leaned into each other.

Epiphany struck her. Victoria's eyes widened. "You can see him?"

Daniel's face slackened as the realization came to him. Surprise spiked his voice. "Yeah, I do. How is that possible?"

She shook her head, unable to provide answers. The

sudden appearance of a brilliant ball of white light spared her the necessity. The spiritual portal appeared directly over the ghostly couple. The gateway rotated and cast dancing rays upon the lovers. It emanated joy and welcome.

Charity broke the kiss. She cupped her husband's face and drew back. "Joseph, my love," she said with tears streaming down her cheeks. "I've missed you so much."

"I'm so sorry. I tried to get back to you but I couldn't—" The frantic apology tumbled from Joseph. He was a fine-looking young man, with sandy brown hair and freckles. He wore a flashy necktie, a cream-colored Homberg hat, and a dapper dark tan suit with pink striping. Joseph lacked the solid definition that Charity possessed. Studying them, Victoria concluded that Joseph was only visible to Daniel while the husband and wife were touching—deriving his substance from her.

"Shh..." Charity shushed him. "It's all right. We're together now. That's what matters."

"I heard you crying—calling to me." Joseph stole another kiss and only Charity's efforts kept it from turning into another long embrace.

"I always knew you hadn't left me willingly. I waited for you." Charity glanced over at Victoria. The spirit's brow pinched with puzzlement. Her lips pursed and she returned her regard to her husband.

"I love you. I love you so much," Joseph declared and at last Victoria concluded that he wasn't even aware of his silent audience.

"I love you too, but the bank's closed." Charity averted yet another amorous advance from her spouse. "We've got to go."

"Go where?" Joseph asked, clearly confused.

The gateway wobbled on its axis, scattering a spray of bright light everywhere—more disco ball than spiritual portal in its bearing. Victoria worried about Charity and Joseph being snatched up and whisked away before the all-important question could be posed. Daniel's arm tightened around her—he shared her concern.

"Charity," Victoria said in a tense voice. "We need to know the location of that gold mine. Our friend went looking for it and he hasn't come back."

Joseph bridled, clearly startled. His head jerked, and he glanced frantically about. "What was that?"

"It's okay, sweetheart." Charity captured her husband's cheeks again. She met and held his gaze. "We can be together now, forever. Just tell me something first. Can you do that?"

His agitation waned. "Yes, of course. I'd do anything for you."

"I need to know about the treasure map you had to the lost gold mine."

Joseph's face reddened. "Ah, Cheri. You know that old thing was baloney."

Charity stilled—deadly serious. "That wicked man murdered you for that map, Joey. Tell me how to find the gold mine."

"All right." Joseph squared his shoulders. "The closest landmark is Slaughterhouse Gulch. Two creeks feed it—branching northwest and northeast. The mine was located in a deep canyon along the northeastern arroyo about two miles from the Slaughterhouse Gulch headwaters. I'm sorry. That's all I know."

"Thank you, my love. That's exactly what we needed." Charity feathered a quick kiss over her husband's mouth and then shot a questioning glance toward Victoria.

Not wanting to disturb Joseph again, Victoria nodded and mouthed her thanks. While it wasn't as ideal as a longitude and latitude, the directions were more than they'd had before. It'd have to be enough to go on.

The couple kissed again. The portal above them brightened in a blinding flash. Reflexively, Victoria shut her eyes and turned her face away. Heat washed across her skin, and a clean, sweet scent—lilacs and plums. She waited until the blaze died down before she looked again. Charity and Joseph were gone. Her breath hitched, and she reached up and found her cheeks were wet with tears. She'd witnessed the crossing over of countless spirits and escorted a number to Valhalla, but this counted as one of the most marvelous and truly touching ascensions ever. It left her wondering, just an inkling in the back of her mind, about the identity of Charity's mysterious benefactor.

"That was amazing. I'm glad we were able to help them." Daniel stepped away from Victoria and stooped to pick up the crowbar. "I'll make sure someone collects Joseph's remains and sees to it he's interred with Charity, but we're running out of time, especially if he's fallen into a haunted gold mine that only appears on All Hollow's Eve..."

Victoria nodded. "Let's go find old Mac Guffin."

Chapter Nine

Overhead, the moon was a bright and silvery disk against the black canvas sky. The stars shimmered and winked down upon them, providing ample illumination. Dawn remained a few hours off yet. True solitude. They'd run out of what could be called a proper road some time ago. The bumpy, narrow pathway they'd been following for the last several miles hardly qualified as a path—it bore closer resemblance to a furrow. She'd seen deer trails with more definition.

The Chevelle's wheel hit a pothole that caused the front right wheel to drop. The car veered to the side. Victoria braced herself against her seat and released a sharp huff when the vehicle came to a safe stop.

Behind the wheel, Daniel glanced over and met her gaze. An unspoken thought passed between them—many more jolts like that and they risked becoming stuck or breaking an axle. He shut off the engine and said, "That's it. We'll have to go the rest of the way on foot."

"That's okay. If we're on foot, I stand a chance of picking up Mac's scent." Stretching her arms overhead,

Victoria took a deep breath, tasting the cool air. The surrounding shrubs and trees had a dry aroma that reminded her of a wood pile. Throughout Arizona, areas normally classified as arid were in the midst of a more than decade-long dry spell. She loved the irony—drought in a desert.

"Good idea." He checked his cell phone. The LCD cast its glow upon his face. "There's no signal—I have zero bars."

"I'm not surprised." She joined him at the back of the car. It'd been miles, almost an hour, since they'd passed the last sign of civilization. Now, it was just the two of them. A profound thought—out here in the middle of nowhere, so far from friends and family, with no means of communication. They were not only alone but dependent upon each other for survival.

"If Macan got hurt or stranded, he couldn't have called for help." Daniel opened the trunk and rooted around, extracting a tactical combat flashlight and a rifle from within. He slung the firearm's carry strap over his shoulder. Aside from various non-magical knives and the holstered handgun, he also wore the enchanted knife sheathed within its scabbard on his belt. He had a backpack well stocked with survival supplies.

"Do you think you have enough weapons?" While he had his back to her, Victoria pulled her shirt and her bra over her head. She tossed the garments past Daniel into the trunk and started on her jeans.

He glanced over, aiming his flashlight toward where her clothing had landed. He reached and came up with her bra straps dangling from his fingers. To her surprise, he didn't turn immediately. Instead, he stared as though riveted by the sight of her practical athletic bra. Damn it—talk about missed opportunities. She could've worn a lacy pushup.

Freya giggled. *Next time.*

Victoria rolled a smile heavenward. *Yes, My Lady.*

Next time.

"Victoria?" His voice fluctuated. The intoxicating aroma of arousal accentuated the cardamom notes she associated with his basal odor.

"I'm going to shift to a wolf so I can better track by scent. I'd rather not ruin my clothes so I'm leaving them in the car." She finished peeling off her pants and underwear, and picked up her flip flops too. Rolling everything together, she pitched the bundle into the trunk. It dropped in — a neat slam dunk.

The chilly night air nipped at her bare skin but not too badly. As soon as she undertook the change to her animal form, her comfort would no longer be an issue. As a wolf, she preferred cooler climates. Rather peevishly, she'd always considered the desert to be a habitat better suited to coyotes than wolves, thought she kept such thoughts to herself. No good came from upsetting her parents or packmates with complaints beyond their control.

"Good idea." He cleared his throat and dropped her bra back into the trunk. Reaching overhead with both hands, he closed the lid. "Is it okay if I turn around? I haven't witnessed many full shifts."

A grin split her face. She strangled on her laughter. "Oh, so you'd like to watch? Purely out of professional curiosity, I'm sure."

He snickered. "Yeah, that's it."

"Okay, sure." Victoria shrugged. She wasn't modest or shy — few shape changers were. In fact, she harbored no doubts as to her own attractiveness. Not every man wanted her, but most heterosexual men looked. She had a trim, athletic figure, with a compact torso and the powerful legs of a ballerina. She also possessed the grace of a dancer due to years of formal training.

Slowly, Daniel turned and came to a full stop. His gaze locked on her, a thorough appraisal with the weight of touch. He stroked her curves, creating a controversy of conflicted sensations—heat and chills, immobility and trembling.

"Wow," he drawled.

She flushed with pleasure—loving the attention—but she refused to indulge in excessive vanity. Preening wasn't her style. Settling into a crouch, Victoria pressed her fingertips to the rocky ground. She gathered her energy, preparing to change shapes. Power flowed over her—her skin rippled over shifting muscles—but the transformation started more slowly than normal. The events of the evening had already drained her reserves, and she hadn't eaten since before the fight with the wight. Swallowing a cry of frustration, she raised her hands from the ground. Dirt and small rocks clung to her palms but she ignored the debris, clenching her hands. When she flicked them open again, all her finger bones broke with an audible crunch. It hurt. She grimaced and growled.

"Are you okay?" Gravel crunched beneath Daniel's boots.

"I—" She tried to offer assurance that she was fine, but it hurt too much. Her skin prickled, hot and flushed, unbearably itchy as white fur pushed to the surface. Her ears grew pointed and migrated to high on her head.

"Victoria?" Daniel bent and reached for her.

"Stop." His proximity threatened her while she was at her most vulnerable. She opened her mouth just as her canines erupted and her jaws distended, pushing into a muzzle. No more words. She snarled, baring her teeth.

Daniel froze, hand extended, surprise on his face as though the family golden retriever had taken a mean turn. Thankfully, for his sake and her own, he refrained from making any sudden movements. He sank into a crouch, lowered his arm, and rested his hand on his knee. Unassuming—maybe even reassuring if she allowed herself to consider him a guardian instead of a potential foe.

Victoria surrendered to her wolf and rode out one of the roughest transformations she'd ever endured. The change clanked through her body like falling dominoes—bones breaking, remolding, and healing. Agony—not the good pain she associated with shape shifting.

At the midway point, she gained in height and weight and resembled nothing so much as the classic movie wolfman—the "fighting" form of most wolf shifters because of the additional stature. Her size once again shrank as she progressed toward her canine form.

As a wolf, Victoria wasn't much bigger than most coyotes and smaller than some of the males. Her fur was pure white, unmarred by even a hint of dark guard hairs. Her father liked to tease her that her color was the reason she disliked heat so intensely. "Victory, you are a snow wolf who had the misfortune of being born in the desert," Adair had said and laughed.

Breathing hard, she dropped to her belly, rested her head on her front paws, and lay there while she recovered her strength. Her belly rumbled its hunger. It hadn't been long since she'd last eaten, but the process required an enormous amount of energy. Come morning, she'd be ravenous. She dreaded the prospect of becoming human again—didn't even want to think about it.

Daniel rocked onto his backside, seated beside her, and reached over. He held his hand hovered over her head as though waiting for a protest or permission. She raised her muzzle, whined, and then yawned.

"Man, this has been a Halloween to remember." Daniel chucked and stroked his palm across the top of her skull, trailing his fingers between her ears. "Silky."

With a snort, Victoria clamored to her feet. All right, rest break over—time to get to work. She took a couple wobbly steps, gaining strength as she walked it out. Daniel rose in a smooth motion and trailed her.

"You ready to go?" he asked in a husky voice.

She ruffed in agreement and charged ahead to assume the lead, running with her nose to the ground. It took a few seconds before she caught the scent of another vehicle—rubber ties, recent exhaust—definitely not more than a day old. With an excited yip, she kicked it into high gear and galloped down the path.

"Hey, hold up!" Daniel's footsteps pounded on the dirt as he charged after her. His rough gait jostled the flashlight so the beam of light bounced wildly.

With a wolf's smile, Victoria slowed her pace to an easy jog so he could keep up. She followed the scent markers for about a half mile. At one point she stopped to examine a tire print in a patch of mud. The width and pronounced threads led her to conclude they were tracking a truck or SUV, the obvious conclusion since any vehicle capable of tracking the rough terrain must have had four-wheel drive. Her suspicions were confirmed when they rounded a bend and came upon an abandoned Chevy Silverado.

"This is Macan's truck. At least we know we're on the right trail." Daniel tried the front door but it refused to open. While he worked on the lock, Victoria ran a circuit about the vehicle with her nose close to the ground. She picked up the missing hunter's scent leading away from the pickup.

Bursting with excitement, she woofed and waited. Daniel didn't come. She barked again but lacked the patience to see if he'd attend. Damn it, she really needed to work on the man's obedience training if they were going to hunt together on a regular basis. Irritated, she doubled back to fetch Daniel and found him still trying to jimmy the door.

"Yeah, just give me a second."

"Nnnnooooohhhh..." Victoria bayed, vocalizing her annoyance, a couple octaves shy of a full howl. She darted toward him and placed a sharp nip on the back of his calf. Not hard enough to pierce denim but definitely to be felt.

He jumped and spun around, aiming the flashlight at her. "All right already! I'm coming. Geez, being nagged by a she-wolf..."

She huffed in satisfaction and reared her front quarters. Twisting about, she returned to where she'd picked up the scent, found it again, and hurried along in a roughly northeastern direction. The ground got rougher—steep slopes covered in loose dirt and gravel. For almost a couple miles, give or take, their route ran parallel to the northeastern arroyo that eventually flowed into the headwaters of Slaughterhouse Gulch.

Out of consideration for Daniel, she kept her pace slow and steady. She sought the safest route even when it took them away from the shortest possible route. Fortunately, Macan had done his best to negotiate an easy course so they seldom strayed more than a few yards from his trail.

Capriciously, the scent trail rose along the base of a butte. Victoria ascended at a hard scramble which sent loose debris shooting out from beneath her paws. She worried about making the ascent worse for Daniel who was behind and below her but a glance over her shoulder confirmed the hunter was keeping up.

She paused, giving him a chance to catch his breath. "Ruff."

"Do you think we're getting close?" Daniel asked, panting with exertion.

"Rrruunnoohhh," she said, doing her best Scooby-Dooism. Dog speech was more difficult than she'd imagined.

"Sorry?" Daniel cocked his head and grinned at her, obviously enjoying himself despite the rough going.

"Roh-roh-roo."

"Hey! No need to be rude."

Muttley wound up being much easier to impersonate—she snickered. After a short break, she resumed hiking. The nearer they got to the summit, the more difficult the climb. Behind her, Daniel muttered a few more choice phrases beneath his breath. She caught the general gist—What the fuck had possessed Macan to come out here alone in the first place? She didn't blame the man for his ire, and frankly, she agreed with him.

Cresting a sharp incline, Victoria ground to a sudden halt. A few inches before her front paws, the earth gave way to a precipitous drop off—not the plateau she'd been expecting. She stared at the spot on the ridge that'd been flattened when something—or someone—landed atop it. To her, it looked as though Macan had tripped and fallen, tumbling down the other side.

Daniel stopped beside her and aimed the flashlight at the patch of disturbed ground. Clearly, his conclusion paralleled hers. He cupped his hands to his mouth and shouted—"Macan!" He repeated the call twice more.

His voice carried on the deceptively quiet night. It seemed like they were the only living things around but her sensitive ears read between the sound waves. She detected the too-silent hush of wary prey become aware of predators in their midst.

"Damn." Daniel lowered his hands and took a step forward.

A man's hoarse voice cried out across a great distance. "Hey! I'm here! Don't leave!"

They exchanged an urgent glance and then scrambled to peer over the crest of the hill. Their combined weight sent an alarming amount of dry earth tumbling down the slick slides of the mount. It was fifty feet down at least.

Daniel called out. "Macan!"

"Yeah! I'm down here!" A second later a red flare shot into the air, illuminating the sides of a canyon below. "Danny, is that you?"

"Yeah, it's me—"

"Oh, hell. I've never been so happy to hear another

person's voice."

"Victoria Storm is with me. Hang in there. We're coming."

"Watch that last step!" Macan croaked, barely audible. "...a doozy."

With a howl of enthusiasm, Victoria leapt over the summit and plunged headlong down the other side. She took it at breakneck speed. Her front paws crashed into the slope, bringing down an avalanche of rubble. Her rear feet touched earth and she rode the cascade for several paces before she pushed off again. The miniature landslide gathered volume as it progressed along the hill.

Her footing remained deft the entire descent—a predator's surefootedness and strength. She was free of fear—even a severe fall couldn't kill her. Broken bones healed at an accelerated rate. But even then, she noticed her own depleted reserves. The evening, including the wight fight and two shifts, had drained her energy. She verged on exhaustion. It concerned her but there was no opportunity for such indulgences. The humans worried her more. The difficult descent would be dangerous for Daniel. She hoped he had the sense to proceed with caution. Ideally, she should have stayed with him but Macan sounded as though he was in serious distress.

She arrived at the bottom of the slope amid a landslide of loose earth. Bounding along at a full run, she found herself heading straight for the opposite side of the canyon at an alarming rate. She dug in her claws, entering an uncontrolled skid in her effort to avoid a head-on collision with the rock wall. She spun in a full rotation, skating on the tips of her nails, and pulled out only to find herself barreling straight at Macan—a flash of gray bristle attached to a beastly huge man.

"Fur fuck's sake!" The old-timer flapped his arms overhead, his accent strong in his agitation.

A wolf's chortle built in her chest. Huffing, Victoria

gathered herself and executed a neat leap that carried her clean over Mac. Though, one of his waving hands brushed her rear leg. She landed and executed a tight turn.

By the time she came around, Macan had recovered his sensibilities. His infliction settled into his Americanized-norm. "You're a mad rocket, Lassie, but I'm damn glad to see you. Is Danny on his way down?"

She barked affirmative, assuming it to be true, but left the task of interpretation to Macan. The hunter rested on the ground beneath a camouflage tarp with a backpack beside him. He hadn't made any effort to stand so she walked over to greet him, wagging her tail.

"Hey! Everyone okay down there?" Daniel called out from above.

"Aye, t'was a close call. I almost got trampled!" Macan answered. "My ankle's broken."

"Stay put. I'm coming down."

"Yeah, right. Where else am I gonna go?"

"What's that?" Daniel asked.

"Naw, never mind!" Macan swept his arms wide in exasperation. "Hurry! The beast might come back at any time."

Beast? Victoria spun in a slow circle, seeking any sign of another creature. But aside from a few insects skittering across the rocky earth, she found nothing. Puzzled, she returned her attention to Macan, wondering if the hunter had hurt his head when he'd fallen. A concussion or dehydration could account for hallucinations, though the man sounded lucid enough. From a hunter, talk of menacing creatures hardly qualified as outside the norm.

Her priorities divided between performing an examination of Macan's injuries and securing the area. Ultimately, concern for external threats won out. The hunter had already been down here for hours. He'd survive another couple minutes until she could get to him.

Besides, Macan and Daniel remained engaged in a shouted exchange of information she was reluctant to interrupt. In passing, she gleaned that Macan believed a menacing apparition inhabited the canyon.

"Hang in there. I'm securing a rope. Beast you say? What'd it look like?"

"I didnae get a good look at it 'cause I was hiding under the tarp. It was big."

"Big?" Whatever he was doing, Daniel's activities sent a rain of loose soil falling into the canyon onto their heads.

"Aye, big."

Victoria performed a thorough inspection of the area, walking a circuit from one side of the canyon to the other—a distance of no more than sixty feet at its farthest point. A conspicuous furrow against the cliff caught her attention. Although it was only a couple feet across, it ran deep—much further back than the other grooves in the gully. Its straight lines had the look of being manmade rather than natural. Thistle bushes and scrubs clung by determined roots from hard-packed earth, forming a curtain of overgrowth. Additionally, the trail was strewn with good-sized rocks.

She picked a path around the debris, navigating it with relative ease thanks to her small size. Her suspicions were rewarded when she located a recessed mine entrance set about twenty feet back. Eureka! Could this be the lost gold mine that so many men had sought and failed to find? She wanted it to be just so she could gloat later.

Three weathered wooden beams formed an irregular entrance—narrower at the top than the bottom. The soil had eroded away, exposing a couple large boulders that overhung the opening. No mine cart tracks or "No trespassing" signs, as many a movie had led her to expect. Still, she considered the discovery really damn cool. As soon as she got the chance—and more urgent matters got dealt with — she intended to show it off.

She doubled back and emerged from the alley just as Daniel completed his descent. He released the climbing rope, took the flashlight from his backpack, and walked toward Macan.

"Damn, Macan — look at you. Do you have any idea what a pain in the ass this is gonna be to explain to my old man?"

Macan huffed. "Don't be a wee clipe! Ye just leave your father outta this. Nuthin's happened here he needs to know aboot."

Head held high, Victoria trotted over to join them. While Macan grumbled, she nudged aside the tarp to get a better look at his legs. A foul odor assaulted her nose. Groaning, she pointed her nose to the side.

"I'm bowfing, Lassie — been down here all day sitting on my bahooky in the dirt beneath thon merciless sun." He obliged her and dragged the cover off his lower legs. His left pant leg had been rolled up and his shoe removed, exposing his ankle which was swollen and bruised.

"Can you heal him?" Daniel asked, stroking his hand from her shoulders to her hips. His touch raised the hairs across her back.

She huffed in exasperation because she lacked the energy necessary to undertake a full shift back to human. Hindsight being 20/20, she regretted her decision to change to a wolf. For tracking and travel, it had been her top choice, but it'd have been really good to be able to communicate with the guys.

Lacking words, she tried the next best thing. "Roof."

"Thon naw or aye?" Macan puzzled. "I dinnae speak woof."

"Not sure," Daniel said, laughing.

"Roof." As her goddess would've said, *Always leave 'em wondering.* Taking a deep breath for fortitude, Victoria leaned in for a closer look. Her eyes cast a goldish glow, illuminating the wound for better viewing, and her professional opinion aligned with Macan's prior conclusion—it was broken. A frustrating development but one they'd have to deal with using traditional first aid. Freya had already forgiven her once for breaking the rules by using her magic to help Daniel. To do so again was simply unacceptable. She refused to cross that line for a man she wasn't intimately involved with.

She glanced up and found both men watching her intently. Her ears flattened against her skull and her tail dropped. With an apologetic whine, she shook her head.

Understanding lit Daniel's face. He clapped his hands. "Okay, looks like we do this the old fashioned way. Macan, let's find some straight branches and get a splint on that leg. We're going to have to make a rig with the ropes and lift you out of here."

"No offense, Danny, but I've got a good hunner pounds on ye."

"It's a good thing we've got a wolf on our side then." Daniel looked straight at Victoria and grinned. She wolf-smiled in return.

"Let's get out of here before that beastie comes back," Macan scolded them with waving arms. Abruptly, he froze. His pie eyes locked upon a distant point and his mouth gaped wide. A bellow erupted from him.

"Ach, ye bastard! 'Mon then, ye hairy bawbag!"

Victoria jerked and pulled back. She opened her mouth to scold the Scotsman but forgot she couldn't speak. Only a rumbling snarl rolled from her muzzle.

"What the—" Daniel also reacted with mixed aggression and confusion. His arms shot up in a defensive stance against the unknown threat.

An eerie green glow appeared behind her and Daniel. She registered movement—shifting shadows—and the brittle crunch of dry dirt. Before she could react, a fist walloped Victoria upside the head. The force of the blow knocked her off her feet and sent her flying. She tumbled through the air.

A cacophony: men's shouts, a piercing, inhuman shriek, and then a rifle boomed.

She smacked into the wall of the canyon and tumbled straight into blackness.

Chapter Ten

Victoria regained consciousness, feeling like she'd gone rounds with a freight train—and lost. Her head throbbed, bloated and burstable, while queasiness swam laps in her gut. Groaning, she twitched her nose and had immediate cause for regret when she snorted a snoutful of dust. She was upside down, muzzle buried in the dirt. Coughing, she slumped over and accidentally pushed into a somersault that sent her rolling ass over teacup. No dignity, but the end justified the means as it righted her so she could breathe properly again.

The effort also brought a whole new sort of suffering in the form of aches and pains. Based on the stabbity-stab in her side and her initial shortness of breath, she had at least a couple broken ribs. She hadn't healed yet and probably wouldn't for some time considering her crippling exhaustion. Mentally, she composed and offered up a fragmented prayer to Freya. Until her regeneration kicked in, she determined to employ careful movement.

Memory returned—Macan and Daniel—and restored her motivation to get back on her feet. No doubt she resembled nothing more than a zombie-wolf as she righted herself on taffy legs. The world swung far to the right—and then returned on a wide arc to the left. Wobbling, she took an experimental step and managed to remain upright.

She lifted her head and glanced about the area in a wary search for the thing that had attacked her. Not just her... Them. She retained a vague recollection of the clash between the hunters and their unknown assailant. Her concern grew urgent—she had no idea how long she'd been out. Apparently long enough for the conflict to play through.

She spied Macan's prone figure on the ground near where he'd been sitting. Daniel was nowhere in sight. Fear for his safety suffocated her. Her protective instincts clamored for her to rush to his rescue. Without a better understanding of what'd happened though, she couldn't do anyone any good. Fighting rising panic, she headed over to investigate.

Reaching the Scotsman, she sniffed him and huffed in relief to discover he was only unconscious, thanks to a nasty injury on the side of his head. If their attacker returned, he was helpless. Her best bet was to hide him. She seized the edge of the tarp in her teeth and dragged it to cover the hunter. Hardly ideal camouflage but he'd said it'd fooled the creature before. Hopefully, it'd work again.

Putting her nose to the ground, she caught the sulfuric scent of a discharged firearm and fresh blood—Daniel's. She searched and found a splatter trail and signs of a person having been dragged into the gulley that dead-ended in the hidden mine entrance. For whatever mysterious reason, the mine monster had chosen to take Daniel while leaving Macan and Victoria behind. Who knew? Maybe it was a random thing. Or perhaps the hunter had seemed like a better prize than an old man with a broken leg or a coyote-sized wolf.

A handgun fired on full auto.

Victoria stopped. The sound originated from deep within the earth, a muffled echo that carried from the craggy opening. She counted five bursts before she recovered her senses and then she stopped counting.

Victoria lunged into action. She dug in her claws, tearing up the soil to acquire traction. Gathering momentum, she shot down the narrow alley, running flat out at her full speed. Lancing pain shot through her side but she bore down with renewed resolve. She locked on the mine entrance—straight ahead of her—with tunnel vision born of single-minded determination.

The firearm's boom ceased—replaced by an otherworldly bellow and a man's combative shout—Daniel. Victoria passed the weathered beams of the mine's ingress. The path sloped downward into the ground. It grew cooler—darker. The rocky sides were narrow and the roof low. Her stride shortened as a matter of necessity to avoid running straight into a wall.

Following the clamor of the battle ahead, she rounded a blind corner and dropped straight into the cold, muddy water of an underground river. Startled, she exhaled a fountain of bubbles but retained enough sense not to inhale. Her feet brushed a rocky bottom, which she used to push off. It sent her shooting upward. The second her head broke the surface, she gulped air and paddled for all she was worth. The depth was about three to three-and-a-half feet. She couldn't touch bottom without diving, which put her at a distinct disadvantage.

A garish green glow lit up the interior of the water-hewn cavern. Victoria cast about for the source, located it, and stumbled into absolute bafflement. She stopped paddling and sank. Her nose submersed, flooding her nostrils with water, and startled her back to her senses. Frantic, she resumed swimming.

When she read Patrick Guffin's journal account of a

giant ghost-skeleton guarding a lost gold mine, she'd naturally taken it with a grain of salt and approached the matter with a healthy degree of skepticism. Guess no one had told *it*.

Old Skelly—a ten-foot-tall skeleton with an unusually thick and heavy bone structure. The water came to its knees and it hunched over because its head and shoulders scraped the ceiling. The thing faced away from her, granting Victoria a clear view of its knobby spine. It held an enormous pickaxe—the kind used in excavation. Stringy pieces of moss clung to its frame. As described in the journal—a copper mine lantern hung suspended within its ribcage, the source of the eerie haze.

She marveled ever so fleetingly at its height—how did it even get around? The mine entrance itself was no more than five feet. She wondered but then she dismissed the stray thought. It didn't matter, and besides, spirits violated the laws of physics with impunity. They had their own unique, discordant rules.

The distinct tap of metal against stone emanated the other side of the cavern beyond the skeleton. Paddling furiously, she managed to raise her head high enough to spot Daniel. The skeleton had the hunter cornered, backed into a crevice in the wall. Their gazes caught for a split second—long enough for her to be certain he'd seen her.

From the looks of it, Daniel had retreated to the only safe place the ghost couldn't reach, but it wouldn't stay so much longer. As she watched, Old Skelly swung the pickaxe overhanded and buried the blade in the fissure, releasing a spray of stone. A big chunk of rock broke off, widening the opening.

Making noise only would've alerted it to her presence, so Victoria approached the fiend, doing her level best to swim stealthily. Despite her efforts, her paws produced noticeable splashing. She got right up behind it. Lucky for her, the ghost had poor perception because it didn't even spare a glance around. It just swung the tool again, laboring to break through.

"I dropped the knife at the entrance to the crevice." Daniel sounded short of breath—he must be wedged in tight. "I can't reach it. Can you distract it?"

Without thinking, she whoofed in affirmation and then cringed. Braced. Waiting for the ghost to turn around, spot her, and smash her to smithereens with the business end of its pickaxe. Once again, it ignored her and she wondered if it was deaf.

At a total loss, Victoria stared at the huge femur in front of her. Her lips peeled past her lips in a silent snarl. Her mouth watered. Before she formulated the thought, her wolf heeded the ancestral calling that said all bones must be bit. Acting on instinct, she seized the thigh bone between her teeth and locked her jaws.

That got its attention. Old Skelly emitted a piercing shriek that filled up the entire cavern. It spun in a fast, furious circle, dragging her through the water. The momentum wrenched her jaws but she hung on with the same stubborn tenacity pit bulls were reputed for.

Around and around she goes—where she stops, nobody knows.

The enraged skeleton never let up, not even for a second. It vocalized its rage—a nerve-shattering screech she swore she would haunt her dreams for years to come. A giant bone hand slapped the water, whacked it again, and then clobbered her. Her head spun, along with the rest of her. Dizzying. Traumatizing her already fragile head and belly.

Fuck him. She refused to let go.

The world wrenched—tilted sideways. The femur in Victoria's mouth flew free and she went with it. She skipped across the pond. Smacked the rock wall. She caught a glimpse of the now one-legged skeleton descending toward her like a felled tree. She yipped in panic but her full mouth muffled the squeak so she sounded like a terrified mouse.

Old Skelly fell on top of her—its central torso aimed at her head. Its spine clobbered her snout, knocking her muzzle aside, and the back of its ribcage formed a cage over her head. The femur in her mouth wedged into other bones, and the whole damn thing sank straight to the bottom of the lake. She landed beneath the skeleton, her side pressed against unyielding rock.

Imprisoned, she plunged into pitch black water, feeling the rise of air bubbles foaming past her. She let go of the femur but found she was trapped in a way that allowed precious little room for negotiation. Her head banged against the lantern suspended within the ghost's ribcage. Despite being submerged in murky water, the lamp continued to glow—lighting the interior of the skeleton's torso so she could make out its individual ribs. Eerie greenness all around.

For a few seconds, she worked her legs at a furious pace, turned and twisted, attempting to escape her prison. Unlike the many things that hurt but didn't kill her, she *could* drown.

Her lungs hurt; her blood pounded in her ears. Her struggles weakened and realization dawned—no matter how hard she fought, she wasn't breaking free on her own. All her exertion only used her remaining air faster. Waiting to be rescued didn't suit her but she had no alternatives except to trust Daniel would find a way to get this thing off her.

Having died once to become a Valkyrie, she had no fear of death... She yearned to live with every fiber of her being. Forlorn and frustrated, she wondered—was this how her life ended? Taken out by a clumsy collection of bones? Oh, the ignominy. Would Freya send one of her sister Valkyries to retrieve her soul, or was she supposed to transport herself? A second death hasn't been covered in the Valkyrie Handbook.

Her chest ached, near bursting. She passed the point

of pain, descending straight into unconsciousness. And where in the name of Hel was Daniel? Had he stopped for lunch?

In answer to her question, the skeleton's dense ribs beside her head shattered inward, forced aside by a thick knife blade. Bone fragments jammed into her face. Victoria flinched and jerked, losing precious air. For a split second, things got brighter because both knife and lantern emanated that same creepy nimbus. But then the weapon's point thrust through the lamp's glass pane and its light expired.

The magic knife's soul-sucking magic drank up the ghost's essence — downing the entire thing in a greedy gulp. It emanated hollowness — emptiness — death.

Her breath exhaled in a rush. Victoria inhaled water. Simultaneously, the prison of bone lifted off her and she was floating free. Blackness filling her inside and out. Distantly, she was aware when big hands seized her and hauled her to the surface. Pressure against her sides — renewed pain from her battered ribs — the expulsion of liquid from her body.

Abruptly, she awoke on the inhalation of a tiny breath, but it wasn't nearly enough. Her body craved more, but her swamped lungs didn't have space. She coughed and vomited muddy water while Daniel held her against his chest, both arms wrapped around her.

"That's it, breathe — just breathe. I've got you. You're safe." Daniel stroked her head, flattening her ears against her skull. His aura sheltered and melded to hers. Ruby tones sparkled like fireworks against the predominant blues which were sapphire bright.

He spoke the truth — in his arms, she was safe. When Victoria whimpered her gratitude, Daniel pressed his face against hers, rubbing his cheek and temple across her snout, and then kissed her nose. She bathed him in wolfy kisses and thumped her tail.

Her hero. They'd have to work on his timing though.

Chapter Eleven

The sun shone bright overhead, nearing its zenith, by the time they finally hauled Macan out of the canyon and back to the Chevelle. During the hour-plus drive back to civilization, exhaustion hung over them, a grim cloud that put a definite damper on the conversation.

The trip to the closest hospital in Prescott passed in relative quiet. Victoria opted to ride in the backseat so the much longer-legged Macan could sit in the front. She crouched, wet and miserable, offensive to her own nose. Shifting back to human had healed her broken bones but required her last iota of strength. The resulting depletion rendered her exhausted—apathetic—grumpy. Even a clean set of clothing failed to help because without a shower, the ick on her skin transferred straight to the cloth.

Thankfully, Daniel put the top up on the convertible so it cut down on the wind noise—not to mention the bug splatter. In the front, the men exchanged only a handful of words. Her drifting mind only registered the low rumble of their voices but not the meaning. The motion of the car created a seductive lull and she nodded off. The next thing she knew, the sound of the car door opening jolted her awake.

"What's happening?" Startled, she bolted upright. Only Macan remained in the front seat. The driver's side was empty. The passenger door was wide open, and Daniel and a young male orderly were helping the Scotsman into a wheelchair.

"It's okay. We're here."

"Did I fall asleep?"

"You were snoring." Daniel leaned over and peeked past Macan at her.

"I don't snore," Victoria returned primly.

"Course not. That racket must've been an elk's mating call."

"Jackass." She glared and threatened him with a closed fist. She fidgeted, eager to exit the vehicle. Being confined didn't sit well with her ravenous, ill-tempered wolf. "I don't snore. What're we doing?"

"We're just dropping off this lazy fool. Then we can be on our way." So saying, Daniel slapped Macan on the shoulder.

"Hey now!" Macan bellowed a good-natured protest and then addressed the orderly. "Heave on three. One, two, three—"

The men uttered cries and groans of exertion but together the three of them managed Macan's bulk from the car to the wheelchair. The metal frame creaked when they plunked him down. They asked the orderly to give them a minute while they formed a huddle.

"You sure about being dropped off?" Daniel asked Macan. "We can come inside with you."

"Oh, nay! I'll be pure dead brilliant. Off with ye!" The Scotsman added rather dourly. "Guess I won't ever learn what happened to my great-grandpappy."

Daniel scowled. "Another time, all right?"

Macan chuckled. "Another time. Thanks, Danny. I widnae made it outta there without ye."

"Sure thing, man. Try to stay out of trouble for twenty-four hours, will you?" Daniel offered his hand and bent over to wheelchair level.

"Aye." The men shook and exchanged a bro hug—lots of heavy back slapping. "Make sure yer father doesn't hear aboot this."

"I'll try to leave your name out of it," Daniel said, laughing.

Victoria kicked her toe against the ground, very much out of place. Frankly, her desires aligned with Macan's. She also preferred that Jake Barrett not hear her name associated with the events that had transpired the day before. It would raise way too many awkward questions.

Sudden movement—the rattling of the wheelchair startled her. She jerked her head, looked up, and found Macan bearing down on her. He stopped and spread his arms wide. "C'mere, wumman. Give old Mac Guffin a hug."

Inexplicably bashful, she wrapped her arm around the big man's shoulders. With him seated, the difference in their heights was inconsequential so she didn't have to bend to reach him. She made a concentrated effort not to jostle his injured leg still wrapped in the makeshift splint.

"Take care, you old coot." She dropped a kiss on the hunter's cheek, brushing her lips across his bristly beard, and crinkled her nose in distaste over his body odor. If possible, his smell was even more offensive than hers.

"Thank you for saving my life, Lassie. Yer a bonnie angel." Macan planted a smooch on her cheek in return, whumped her across the back, and released her.

"You're welcome." She smiled and blushed, flattered and embarrassed all at once. She stepped over to stand beside Daniel and they watched while the orderly ushered Macan through the sliding entrance into the hospital.

Chapter Twelve

Once the Scotsman wheeled out of sight, they turned toward each other. Awkwardness slammed down on top of them. She opened her mouth but said nothing—the words refused to congeal. To her chagrin, Daniel appeared just as uncomfortable. The man scowled like the dickens and also stayed silent.

The two of them were quite the sight. By now, their clothing had dried out in the arid air so the material was now stiff and crusty rather than wet and mucky. Her muscles ached, staying on her feet required effort, and her belly yawned. She was, in short, miserable. Like her, Daniel looked—*and smelled*—the part of a survivor of a natural disaster. The pallor of exhaustion hung over him; his movements slow and trudging.

After everything they'd just been through together, it killed her to be overcome with uncertainty and doubt. She wondered what came next. They'd completed their task, accomplished their stated goal—located and rescued the missing hunter. Beyond that, their next move remained a total blank.

He cleared his throat. "I doubt they'll let us back into

our suite."

A wry smile twisted her mouth. "Yeah. It's not exactly fit for habitation. What about our stuff?"

"I'll make some calls and arrange to recover our belongings. My weapons have probably been confiscated. It'll take some wrangling through official channels to get everything back."

She dipped her chin. "Okay. There's nothing in my bags I can't live without."

"So..." He hung a thumb off his belt and then released it, a telltale gesture. "What do you want to do? If we head straight back to Phoenix we'll be there before two."

"Is that what you want to do?" Victoria bristled, more than a little cagey. So—*this* was how he wanted to end their second unofficial date? If he failed to at least offer to buy her lunch, she swore on Freya's sweet chariot cats—she'd bite him.

He regarded her with savvy appraisal, a wry intelligence that said the man was no fool. "I want to do whatever you want to do."

Smart man. Grumbling, she deliberated for a moment. "I'm starving."

"Break..." He glanced up, noting the time. "Lunch it is then."

"My own stench might kill me before we can eat."

He chuckled. "We'll take care of both. Tell me what you need. What's more important—food or a hot shower?"

"A shower." No matter how hungry, she wasn't in any danger of dying from famine any time soon.

"All right, then."

They returned to the Chevelle. Daniel drove them to a nearby hotel that lacked the Hermosa Inn's historic charm. She hoped it also lacked for restless spirits. From the outside, it appeared clean and well-maintained. The facility consisted of a cluster of two-story buildings with doors facing outward toward railed walkways. It had a fence and an outdoor pool. Normally, she loved swimming but at the moment, the prospect aroused zero interest in her.

While he disappeared into the lobby to check them in, she waited in the car. Daniel returned fifteen minutes later carrying a big, stuffed plastic bag. He proffered it to her without explanation so she wrapped her arms about it and dragged the whole thing into her lap.

"What's this?"

"I told the clerk that the airline lost our luggage."

"Great idea." Victoria peeked inside and found soft white terrycloth—a pair of robes. She dug deeper and found other delights. "Toothpaste—you're a god."

"Thanks, but I try not to let it go to my head."

He parked close to their second-story room and together they trudged up the stairs. As soon as Daniel unlocked the door, Victoria pushed past him. She made a beeline for the bathroom. Within, she shed her soiled clothes, freed her hair from its braid, and jumped straight into a scalding hot shower. Her mood took an immediate turn for the better. She scrubbed herself down from head to toe, washing away the accumulated dirt and dried blood from the hunt. Once she was clean, she stayed there a time, soaking beneath the spray, inhaling the purifying steam which helped clear her airways of the lingering mine filth.

The creak of a bathroom floorboard alerted her to Daniel's presence. The vanity lights backlit his form so his shadow fell across the shower curtain. Excitement coursed through her. Leaving the water on, She tensed and turned to face him through the vinyl drape that separated them.

"I've ordered food. It's being delivered. I hope that's okay."

"It's great. Thank you." She hit the shutoff. "Will you pass me a towel, please?"

"Sure." A rustle accompanied his movement. "Here you go—"

A washcloth appeared over the top of the shower bar, dangling from his fingers. Victoria stared at it. Squinted. Her lips quivered and then turned up in an involuntary smile. She fought and failed to suppress laughter, but the effort turned the sound she produced into a brassy giggle-snort.

"Very funny." She snatched the washcloth from his fingers, grabbed the shower curtain, and drew it aside. To her immense disappointment, he faced away from her—and held a bath towel in his other hand—just above his backside.

"Sorry, I couldn't resist," Daniel said, but the man didn't sound apologetic in the least. In fact, he was downright smug. Belatedly, it occurred to her to look past him to the vanity. Steam fogged the mirror but only partially thanks to the cold air streaming in through the open doorway. He still had a damn fine view.

"I bet you couldn't." She took the towel from him and smacked his ass for good measure. The whack elicited an appreciative chuckle from him. Without being told, he vacated the bathroom.

She dried off and put on the white robe he'd left on the counter. It claimed to be one-size-fits-all but the enormous thing engulfed her. The bottom fell to her ankles but it was clean and soft—she loved it. Five minutes later, she emerged with waist-length hair loose about her shoulders. Unfortunately, the hotel had only supplied a comb so she anticipated it'd take forever to work through the kinks.

She found Daniel waiting for his turn to use the bathroom, a folded robe clutched in hand. He had the right idea. His hygiene hadn't fared any better than hers. Before she'd showered, her own stench had masked his, but now that she had... Her nose scrunched in distaste.

"Can I get in there now?" The look on Daniel's face

conveyed—*Yeah, I get it. You don't need to rub it in.*

Victoria snickered. "It's all yours."

"Thanks." He disappeared within and closed the door behind him. She listened but detected no click to indicate it'd been locked. A few seconds later, the shower came back on.

Victoria waited a full minute before she crept to the bathroom, eased the door open, and sneaked inside. Sly as a fox, she snatched up every single clean towel except for a single washcloth, which she generously left behind on the rack. Clutching her prizes, she returned to the main room where she dropped the stack on the bed and flopped down beside it. With a sigh of pleasure, she rolled onto her back, luxuriating the scent and slide of fresh linens.

She listened to the muffled water flow which meant the shower was still in use. She was more tired than she thought because she drifted. Distantly, she dreamed Daniel called out her name in a soft voice. She may have murmured something in reply or maybe not. The next thing she knew, the mattress heaved with the addition of a heavy male form seated upon the edge of the bed. A mouth-watering aroma yanked her straight out of slumber.

"Wake up, sleepyhead. The food is here."

On cue, Victoria's stomach rumbled. Blinking, she sat straight up and looked around. True to Daniel's word, three large white sacks bearing the logo of a Mexican restaurant sat on the table—the source of the delicious scent. Her wolf burst over her, and it required an act of will to quell the desire to vocalize her exuberance for food. The situation so richly deserved a joyous yodel.

"How long was I asleep?"

"Less than an hour." Daniel rose and crossed the room. He wore a robe that was identical to hers except the hemline stopped at his knees. The white terrycloth offset his deep tan. Curiosity led her to cast a quick glance at her own arm, confirming that the man was a couple shades darker.

He flashed a slow smile. "That was a low blow—taking all the towels."

"Yeah? Well you had it coming."

Sharing a laugh, they dragged the only chairs in the room over to the small round table. Conversation remained at a minimum while they dug out and distributed the food across the surface. From the looks of it Daniel must have ordered half the menu—burritos, enchiladas, tamales, and tacos. Snatching up a Styrofoam container at random, Victoria pried open the lid off, releasing a cloud of steam straight into her face. She inhaled—tasting the vapor—and identified the spicy stew as birria—goat stew.

Her startled gaze flew to Daniel. "You didn't—"

"I figured it might make up a bit for you having missed the Winter Nights feast." He passed her tortillas and a spoon.

"Thank you." Speechless, she got down to the serious business of feeding her wolf, though real wonderment lingered in her mind. Granted, consuming goat meat stew hardly equated to performing the ritualized sacrifice in honor of the Vanir deities—Freya and her brother, Freyr. But the sentiment carried a lot of weight. It amazed and impressed her that he'd been so attentive to what mattered most to her.

Freya chimed in, *It is a worthy gesture. Grant him my appreciation and thanks.*

I will do that. Swallowing a mouthful, Victoria wiped her mouth on a napkin. She watched Daniel down the end of a burrito. "Freya desires that I convey her appreciation and thanks."

A smile tugged at his lips. "You're welcome. I hope this makes up some for what was probably the crappiest second date in the history of the world."

She chortled. "Oh-ho-ho! So you finally admit this was a date?"

"Yeah. You've got me."

"It wasn't so bad. I got to spend time with a really great guy—and fight the ghost of a giant skeleton. How many women can say that?"

"Not too many." He smiled but his expression remained pensive.

"What's wrong?"

"I'm wondering whether there's going to be a third date."

Oh. Damn. Victoria's teeth sank into her lower lip, and she worried it. She harbored more than a few reservations about the appropriateness or workability of *them*—a wolf and a hunter. Oh, as allies and hunting partners, they made a sublime team. But romantically? She had her misgivings.

Daniel noted her lack of ready response with a wry smile. "Yeah, that's what I was afraid of."

"I'm sorry. I'm not sure if this is a good idea."

"What is it you're not sure about? At least give me a chance to change your mind." He pushed aside the containers and shoved away from the table, dragging his chair closer to hers.

"It's not about changing my mind... It's not made up one way or the other. We make a good team when it comes to hunting but this—" She turned her hand in a vague gesture which conveyed the murkiness of her emotions.

"We do more than just fight well together. We're good together, period. I know you've got doubts. You're always holding back—watching me—judging me. But I have no idea what you're thinking."

She found herself caught in a quagmire of awkwardness. Impulsively, she opted for humor as a means of defusing the tension. Deliberately comical, she leered at his chest. "Most of the time I'm just lusting after all those muscles."

"Thanks, I think." He laughed and she sighed.

"You're right. I have some reservations."

"Let's talk about it. C'mon, it's only fair for you to tell me what's holding you back. I can't convince you if you won't talk to me."

"I'm talking. I'm just not sure what to say."

"Bullshit. You always know what you want to say. You hold your tongue when you're being diplomatic."

She stared at him in astonishment. "When did you get to know me so well?"

"Are we back to this being a hunter-wolf thing?"

"No," she snapped. "We're back to this being a respect thing."

He jerked and drew back. "I respect you.

"Do you?"

"Yeah, I do." Daniel's eyes narrowed; the rest of his face hardened. His stance underwent a pronounced transformation to assertive, and his scent soured on the strident rush of anger. She'd insulted his honor.

Visceral delight thrilled through her. She tensed in response to his aggression—capitalized on it. She wanted him angry and invested in their relationship—if that was truly what *this* was. "Then why didn't your family accept my mother's offer to heal your mom when she fell ill?"

Surprise wiped out his ire. His eyes hooded, and his lips parted but he hung onto his words with grim greed. Innate caution led him to consideration—and contemplation, both of her and the issue. She approved of his discipline—restraint carried weight with her. A taciturn man seldom had cause to regret his words. And a man who couldn't control his temper lacked the mettle to make a good Alpha.

Lesser males weren't worthy of her.

"Believe me, if it'd been up to my father, my brothers, and me, we would have. But it was my mother's call.

She refused magical intervention." He flexed his hands, telegraphing his tension.

"Why? Why would she—" A startled exclamation escaped Victoria. Of all the potential answers he might've given, she wasn't expecting *that*. She cut herself short because the question was both intrusive and insensitive. *None of her damn business.*

Daniel smiled, tight and grim. "Believe me, we asked the exact same thing. My father was furious. He and mom got in a shouting match—my parents never argued. At least, not in front of us."

"I'm sorry." Guilt crushed her, condemning her own narrow-minded assumptions and prejudices. It served her right for making snap judgments. Ever since she'd been little, her father had cautioned Victoria, citing her tendency to do so as a barrier to someday taking over leadership of the pack.

"Don't apologize." His piercing gaze conveyed the unsettling impression that the man could read exactly what she was thinking. "My family understands that wolves don't share their magic with outsiders. I don't know whether it was properly expressed at the time, but we appreciated the offer. We're grateful."

Relief washed over her. Maybe, just maybe, Jake Barrett wouldn't oppose Victoria dating his oldest son as strongly as she'd feared. And she despised the fact she even cared what Daniel's father thought. But damn it, the man exerted influence like a black hole—even in his absence, his sway affected everyone and everything for light years around. She worried about unforeseen consequences to herself and her pack if she chose to pursue a relationship with the Hunter King's eldest son.

"You can speak for your father on that?" Victoria asked, needing to be sure.

"I speak for my father on the matter," Daniel said. "Dad thanked your parents at my mom's funeral."

"I didn't know." She hadn't attended the funeral because the invitation only extended to her parents. However, his words had the ring of conviction—and the scent of it. Truth. And she considered him a man to be taken at his word. Victoria smiled, content, and dismissed the matter—and her doubts.

His unwavering gaze pierced her defenses, seeing past all her facades. "Are we good now?"

An involuntary smile split her mouth. "Yeah, we're good."

They rose in concert, smoothly as through a practiced maneuver. But thanks to her diminutive height she beat him to it. The food still smelled plenty inviting, but the birria she'd consumed had taken the edge off. She hungered still—but for other things.

Sliding toward him, she raised her hand and pressed her palm against his bare chest where the robe split. Smooth skin over firm muscle. His heart beat strong and steady—a cadence to put her faith in. She parted the material, exposing the tattoo over his heart. Ever so lightly, she feathered her fingers over the two words— *Absit omen.*

"What does this mean?" Victoria asked.

"*Absit omen*—may what is said not come true." His smile was strange and quirky, as though the man had a secret he wasn't sharing. She scented evasion if not outright deception. She suspected him of leaving a lot unsaid. And that was okay. He'd explained enough to satisfy her curiosity.

She liked an intriguing hint of mystery in a man.

"Is that a blessing or a curse?" She scraped her nails across his pecs, deliberately grazing his flat nipples—he tensed beneath her touch.

"A bit of both? I'm not entirely sure sometimes." Daniel's gaze locked on her face, his pupils fully dilated. Unmissable arousal permeated his aroma—notes of toasted spice and rich earthiness—all him except for the lingering hint of soap and the hotel's complimentary citrus shampoo.

"It's a ward against possession," she surmised. During the fight at the hotel, the wight had tried so hard to enter him but hadn't even been able to get a foothold—this explained why.

Fleeting surprise crossed his face. "Yeah, it's a ward against involuntary possession."

But it allowed voluntary possession? She licked her lips, tempted to ask, but thinking about other things. So apparently was he, because he bent and captured her lips in a ravenous kiss. He wrapped his powerful arms around her, caressing her back through the terrycloth. Reaching up, she clung to his broad shoulders and stood on her toes. Their mouths merged, tongues stroking. The all-too-evident proof of his desire tented the front of his robe.

Too much clothing. With a whimper of frustration, she caught his wrist and guided his hand beneath the V-neckline to her small, firm breast. His rough palms covered her completely and abraded her nipple. Liquid heat coursed through her.

"Oh, baby." Daniel's breath escaped in a slick hiss. The air thickened with the musk of his spiked arousal. He claimed her mouth in a kiss of crushing gravity—irresistible attraction.

In a coordinated motion, they scuttled the three feet to the edge of the bed and tipped over into it, landing with an energetic bounce that broke their kiss. Laughing, she rolled over so she faced him. Daniel propped his head on his hand, a devilish little smile on his lips. His breath ghosted over her face; firm lips feathered across her temple. Victoria inhaled and stirred in his arms but held back. She didn't want to rush—too lazy and too content. Their first time together was special and should be savored.

"Mmm, you smell good." She stroked her hands across his bare chest. She extended her leg to brush his bare calf—coarse, springy hairs beneath the pads of her bare toes.

"So do you."

"There's something I need to know..."

"What's that?" Daniel asked, foggy and distracted.

"Whether you're compensating..."

"What?" He frowned in clear confusion.

Victoria tried and failed to suppress giggles—she erupted into a girlish fit. As bold as she pleased, she slipped her hand past the part of his robe and captured his cock, wrapping her hand about the heavy base. His thick length pressed against her palm and the inside of her wrist... Her grin widened.

He groaned, leaning into her touch. "Am I compensating?"

"We'll see." Victoria coached her tone to snarky. "I was taught growing up, it's not what you've got but what you do with it." She rolled him onto his back and threw a leg over him, straddling his thighs.

A squawk of dismay escaped her when he flipped them using an unexpected wrestling move. He shoved her robe aside and slid down her body, the hot exhalation of his breath playing across her skin. He kissed and licked her navel. She moaned, coherent thought destroyed, reduced to a quivering mass of need.

Daniel chuckled. "And I was taught—ladies first."

The End.

About the Author

Melissa Snark is a paranormal and romance author with a particular interest in werewolves and Norse mythology. Her Loki's Wolves series combines elements of both in a contemporary fantasy setting. She lives in Northern California with her husband, three children and a glaring of cats.

www.ingramcontent.com/pod-product-compliance
Lightning Source LLC
Chambersburg PA
CBHW050542190726
48284CB00003B/1183